Mr Adamson

THE
SEAGULL
LIBRARY OF
GERMAN
LITERATURE

Mr Adamson

URS WIDMER

Translated by Donal McLaughlin

LONDON NEW YORK CALCUTTA

This publication was supported by a grant
from the Goethe-Institut India

Seagull Books, 2019

Originally published as *Herr Adamson* by Urs Widmer
© Diogenes Verlag AG Zürich, 2009. All rights reserved.

First published in English translation by Seagull Books, 2015
English translation © Donal McLaughlin, 2015

ISBN 978 0 8574 2 716 8

Typeset in Cochin by Seagull Books, Calcutta, India
Printed and bound by WordsWorth India, New Delhi, India

Yesterday was my ninety-fourth birthday. We celebrated as we always do on birthdays. Susanne had baked a chocolate cake, a Sachertorte, or, rather, a rustic variation, the recipe for which my mother had inherited from her grandmother. It has survived two world wars and the Great Depression. Noëmi, our daughter, who loves everybody's birthdays, just not her own, tried like every year to put as many candles as possible on the cake. This time she found space for about fifty (she bought the tiniest possible) on the approximately one hundred square centimetres of cake. You could hardly see the chocolate. It had been ousted by the candles, probably. The other forty-four were in concentric circles around the cake. Content, Noëmi looked at her work and said, 'But don't live to a hundred, Papa. That's as many candles as I can manage.' — It wasn't so easy to light them. One close to the centre still wouldn't light when all the ones at the periphery were long ablaze. And at the periphery, while Noëmi was busy with the last of the candles, the first were already going out. Noëmi, at any rate, burnt her fingers a few times. Finally, they did all glow together. It looked like something to do with a Nordic Midsummer Night celebration, or like some magical Mayan icon. 'Ah!' and 'Oh!' we exclaimed before blowing out the candles. I managed roughly none, Susanne two or three, Noëmi about twenty and Anni, my granddaughter, now long since grown up too, the rest. Or, rather, her two boys helped her, their puffed cheeks blowing hard across the fire. The smoke, once the blaze was extinguished, filled the entire room. I was coughing, Susanne, rubbing her runny eyes; Noëmi opened all the windows, Anni laughed and the boys shrieked. We beamed at one another happily. Each of us got a piece of cake with a dozen candles on it—the stearin had melted into the chocolate. We'd some chewing to do. I unwrapped my presents: a miniature boat, a bark, with a black ferryman at the stern with an oar in his hands (from Susanne); a gingerbread heart with 'Bon voyage' written on it (Noëmi); a loaf of bread that smelt wonderful and a bottle of wine (Anni). The two boys—twins who have modern names of some sort but we all call them Bembo and Bimbo—had done a drawing for me in which a man (with my features, so, a moustache and wild hair on either side of a bald head) was walking towards the horizon over which a red sun was shining. I hugged the three women, in order of age, and the two boys. Freeing themselves, they shouted — as they always do when they visit, 'Are you coming out to play, Great-Granda?' And like every time, I went out to play with them. Almost always, we play cops and robbers — we did this time, too — as Bembo and Bimbo are highly gifted cops with thundering voices and I'm a good thief as I can still run, like Carl Lewis back in the day, a hundred metres in ten-point-zero. Minutes, I mean. Not seconds.

When I first met Mr Adamson I was eight. In the garden of Mr Kremer's villa, it was. The villa was across from our house and not a villa at all — everyone just called it that — but a modest building with two floors, albeit with a very big garden around it. The unusual thing was that Mr Kremer was never at home. Ever. No one had ever set eyes on him, and on no one else either. No wife, no children, no servants, no gardener. The garden looked as you might expect. A florid virgin landscape that no one could see for a thick boxwood hedge surrounded the house and the garden. A large gate with a serious iron plate prevented access. A bell that remained silent when, on one occasion, I did dare to press it, ready to vanish in a flash into *my* garden. The one around Mr Kremer's villa was, of course, much more exciting. It was forbidden territory, Mr Kremer might inflict terrible punishments if he were ever to turn up and find me standing in the middle of his secret. Me and Mick, that is. Mick was my friend and—like me—knew every corner of this enchanted lair where we moved as alert as lynxes and as wary as gazelles, full of fear, full of desire, at all times prepared—amid all this magnificence—for disaster to strike.

That day—it was my birthday then too, my eighth, as I say, and the sun was shining just as warmly as it did yesterday—I entered the garden, as always, through a narrow gap between the boxwood hedge and the high wall that was the dividing line between this property and that of the white lady. The white lady—that is another story. Let me tell you this much—she always (and I mean *always*) had white clothes on. White shoes, white gloves, white hat. All around the house and in her rhododendron garden she'd had alarms installed, trip wires, sensors, sirens she set off three or four times a day. With a shrill voice, she'd then report to the onrushing police that she'd seen a shadow, a whole army of shadows, all after her blood. With a bit of luck, she won't appear in this story—which is about Mr Adamson—again.

In the garden, the grass grew navel-high and wherever you looked flowers were rampant. That particular day — back then, I didn't know the names of the flowers whereas now I do — red and white roses were in bloom (at the front gate), poppy, oleander, hibiscus, long-stemmed marguerite (thousands of them), hydrangea (a cemetery flower that, here, looked cheery and southern), clematis, meadow sage, lavender, phlox, snapdragon, campanula, geranium (frightful flowers when they hang in the windows of chalets in Berne; they too beamed with red pride), fuchsia, blackthorn, azalea, wisteria, thyme, rosemary and honeysuckle (this was rampant in a distant corner of the garden where, beyond the boxwood hedge, there was a bench at which walkers occasionally stopped for rest). Birds twittered, sparrows, blackbirds, tomtits, finches, robins. From a distant forest a cuckoo cuckooed. Lizards darted off, butterflies joggled in the air. I stood there, entranced, more so than ever as I was actually an Indian and Indians know no pain. And so no frenzied celebrations either.

I sniffed around a little like an Indian, analysed tracks (flattened grass) and pursued my own as if a stranger had left them. Without Mick, it wasn't quite as exciting. I've forgotten where Mick was that day. At school probably — he was two years older (stronger too, but I was sharper off the mark) and had lessons even on my free afternoons. He also often had to stay behind after school for leaving all his homework at home or not doing it at all. So I beheaded all the marguerites with a stick and sneaked—with my fingertips to the ground and my eyelids half shut so the brightness of my eyes couldn't be seen—to the corner of the garden as the voices of two or three women could now be heard from there. With the greatest of caution I pushed my way through the grass until I was lying beneath the boxwood hedge, not breathing, almost, and right behind the bench. I could have reached out and touched the back of it. The three women I could only see from behind—for there were three—were old and had probably run away from the old people's home at the bottom of the street. With their loud, high voices, they were talking about their problems with their bladders, their bowels and their brains. It was like in a game of poker—if one of them had a *full house* (a stone as large as your fist blocking her kidney and laying the lady low with unspeakable pain), another turned out to have a *royal flush* (bowel cancer, inoperable) and so won.

I retreated backwards, just as cautiously, restoring every blade of grass to its original position so that no one, not even the most cunning lookout of the Kiowa tribe, would notice anything unusual. After only a few metres, that had already become boring, so I got up and walked to the bench at the wall of the house. I sat down, sang 'Hark! What is that sound I hear?' and stared at the sky where two birds of prey were circling.

Mr Adamson appeared before me so suddenly, it was as if he'd fallen to earth. I got a terrible fright. I was sure he was Mr Kremer, the invisible lord of the house and the garden, and that all the fires of hell were about to burn me. I remained seated, as if superglued to the bench.

'Good afternoon,' I said, finally.

'And there was me thinking you were someone else after all,' he said and laughed. He spoke standard German, not the German we speak around here, and did so with an oddly strange melody. 'I was beginning to think you couldn't see me. Allow me to wish you "Happy Birthday".'

'How do you know it's my birthday?'

'Well, it's mine in a way too today.' He laughed again. His laugh sounded parched, like a cough almost. No one laughed like that around here. In the desert perhaps, in the heat of an erupting volcano.

'Are you Mr Kremer?' I asked.

'Adamson,' he said, with a little bow. 'Mr Adamson.' It was as if he sang his name.

I could feel myself getting less scared-stiff. I didn't say anything else and Mr Adamson too looked around the garden in silence. 'It's great here,' he muttered. 'A bit bright.' He put a hand over his eyes to shade them but the sun was still dazzling him. Despite that, he looked here and there and up at the sky. 'It's time we got to know each other.— What a beautiful garden!' Indeed. Now that I was following Mr Adamson's gaze, the garden suddenly looked as if a gardener with really green fingers took care of it. All this beauty couldn't just be a freak of nature. Maybe Mr Kremer came at night when I was asleep and pottered around secretly in this paradise of his.

Mr Adamson—if he wasn't Mr Kremer after all, I needed to be on my guard still—was old, ancient, about ninety probably, small, thin, and he had a very white head with a pointy nose and an even pointier upper lip that came out over his lower lip and chin like a porch. He was completely bald if you ignored the three single hairs that, one behind the other and with a slight curl, grew out of his head. They looked like aerials or three blades of yellow grass. He was wearing a grey cardigan, not right for the time of year, somehow colourless trousers and brown socks. No shoes.

'So you're an Indian,' he said, serious this time, pointing at my hair. I had indeed—as I always did when I forced my way into the garden of Mr Kremer's villa—put my Indian feather in my hair. I'd found it in the forest. No idea what bird it was from.

'From the Navajo tribe.' I looked at Mr Adamson proudly. 'I'm a chief. Running Deer. My friend Mick is the other chief. Wild Storm is his name.'

Mr Adamson went over to the roses and smelt them. It was as if he was floating, you could hardly see where he'd walked, here and there a flattened blade of grass, a crushed marguerite, I could be mistaken about even that though. Maybe *I*'d done that.

'Wonderful!' he called across from the gate. 'I guess they have a nice scent?' He stuck his nose into a bloom and laughed. 'Oh well,' he said. Whistling cheerfully, he came back to the bench and joined me, leaving space between us.

'Whatever happened to Kimmich, the shoemaker, really?' he asked.

'A shoemaker called Kimmich? There's no shoemaker called Kimmich around here. Ours has a shop in Tellstrasse and his name is Brzldrzk or Orzlhmsk. A name that's not from here. He'd a hard time, my father says, during the war and is now all alone in his shop. No wife, no children, only shoes. Everyone's dead, where he comes from.'

'During the war?' Mr Adamson said. 'What war would that be?'

'*The* war. Wasn't it wartime for the longest time? I even saw, from the roof of Mick's house, how the Yanks shot down a German plane. Or the Germans one of the Yanks. It was far away but we could see the trail of smoke. It crashed down like a rock. On one occasion, a piece of shrapnel went into the wall of the house, right next to Mick's father's head. He told Mick they weren't even allowed to shoot here, against all international law it was. But they do it anyway. He looks a little like you, incidentally, Mick's father. Has an upper-lip porch too. Except, he's younger and always has a pipe in his mouth.'

'I used to smoke too,' Mr Adamson said, smiling. 'Cigars. Havanas. From Cuba, they were. — It's quite normal actually, what you say about Mr Kimmich. I lived in Tellstrasse back then too. He must have given up the shop. He wasn't much younger than me.'

'Tellstrasse was bombed. Don't you know that?'

'I used to live there,' Mr Adamson said.

'I heard the blasts here in the garden and cycled down on my mama's bike. Smoke everywhere. My papa was seriously annoyed and — when I finally got home — almost cuffed my ear. He hugged me so hard, I nearly suffocated. — Was that your house that was damaged?'

'Don't know,' Mr Adamson said. 'Didn't I say so already?'

'Well, the very first house is the one I mean. At the station, nearly. I looked into the rooms. In one, a piece of floor was still hanging. There was a lamp on it. It was the only bombing in this town. — They chucked down a few bombs in Zurich too, and in Schaffhausen. That was too far for me though, with the bike.'

'Can you keep a secret?' Mr Adamson said.

'Of course!' I exclaimed. 'Mick and I have a secret, I've sworn to him on the soul of the Manitou of all Navajos never to tell it to anyone, anyone at all, and it's a terrible secret. Mick was in the park and a man was behind a tree with a really red prick, it was *so* big, huge and as red as blood, Mick said, and he ran away, and now that's our secret. When I told my mother, she said I'm not allowed ever ever ever to speak to a man I don't know. So as you can see, I can keep a secret.'

'Hmm,' Mr Adamson said, looking at me pensively. 'Our secret is: you're not allowed to tell your mama you've met me. Not your papa. Nor Mick. Agreed?'

I nodded. I wanted to hit his chest with my fist, like Mick and I did when we made important decisions but he stepped back.

'We'll see each other another time,' he said. 'It really is beautiful, this garden.—Look over there. A bird with golden feathers.'

'Where?'

'There, on the hedge.'

I looked over. There was no golden bird, not even an ordinary one. I turned back to Mr Adamson. But he was gone. Had vanished without a trace. I looked to the left, I looked to the right, I looked behind me and up into the sky. Nothing. So I got up and toddled off home.

I called Mick Mick and he called me Mick. He was me and I was him. The next morning, early, as early as boys bursting with energy like to be, I ran across the field between my house and his and, without knocking, opened the door to the building and then the apartment and charged into the kitchen. It must have been a Sunday, everyone was at home in my family—my mama, my papa and my big sister and my little sister too—and in Mick's kitchen too, Mick's mother *and* Mick's father were in the same place. Something that was exceedingly rare. Mick was sitting at the table and holding a gigantic cup up to his lips. 'I'm coming. I just have to finish my milk first.' His hair was bristling at the thought, he couldn't stand milk. If he drank it quickly, he got sick, and if he sipped it slowly, it made everything worse because then a thin skin formed on top, causing him no end of nausea. *That* was why his mother was standing beside him, not letting him out of her sight. She was convinced that milk was healthy and that Mick was capable — and she was absolutely right about this — of emptying the contents of the cup down the sink if she took her eyes off him for even a second.

I said, 'I'm waiting!' and sat down opposite him. Mick lifted the cup again — his face vanished behind the gigantic pot that you could have watered an elephant with — but his drinking noises sounded more like he was filling the milk in his stomach back into the cup. His mother watched sceptically and his father, not in the least aware of the drama playing out before his very eyes, refilled his pipe.

Mick's name was Hanspeter, everyone but me called him Hanspeter. Just as I was called by my Christian name at home and in school. Mick's mother was wearing a blue flame-patterned dress with lots of antique pink silk ribbons hanging down her body like seaweed, and warbling away

13

to herself, as she always did, fragments of an unrecognizable melody, interrupting herself only to say 'Well done!' or 'You see?' to Mick. He was still making the same noises. Mick's mother liked to sing and put on make-up even when she was at home. Mick's father—who now said 'Back to work then!', sucked at his pipe, blew out the smoke, nodded to me and went back into his study—was a professor, a professor of beetles. A coleopterist, as I would say nowadays. His study was full of cases with skewered beetles. Small ones, big ones, a few huge ones. Green, brown, black, spotted, golden. Mick's father sat all day long at a huge table full of microscopes, bowls, bottles, beetles, fountain pens, blank and written-on papers, magnifying glasses. A tin full of pencils of every colour. A large basket with at least a dozen more pipes. Once a week he went to the university and taught his students the difference between the Carabidae, the Anobiidae and the *Leptinotarsa decemlineata*. The Carabidae ran, the Anobiidae knocked and the *Leptinotarsa* squatted on the potato leaf and gobbled it up. Mick's father never sang but played records indiscriminately and at a booming volume from early in the morning until late at night. Monteverdi, Bix Beiderbecke, Gesualdo, Beethoven, Buddy Bertinat and his Orchestra, Dvořák. With no artistic ambition whatsoever and absorbed in the analysis of the leg of a stag beetle, he whistled along to the melodies. Something really booming was playing right now. Mick's mother warbled on, paying no attention to the beats of the drum from the next room.

(My parents—just as an aside—were normal. My mama was as broad as she was tall, the shape of a globe, warm, the smell of good milk. My whole head could vanish between her breasts. She liked to laugh and chatted a lot. My papa was a taciturn man and more serious than my mama. He was of slight build, scrawny almost—but still a giant in my eyes—and worked for the electric company in town. In some way or other, he made sure the lights didn't go out, how exactly I don't know to this day. Whether he inserted or took out fuses, or whether he had a higher position and, from a control panel, readjusted the power lines if there was the danger of a power cut because once again, up at the Gotthard, a tree had crashed onto the high-voltage power transmission line. He always wore an overall anyway.

Each evening when he came home, he would open a bottle of beer—a karate chop to the clamp, he always succeeded at the first attempt—and have a long gulp. He would sigh with relief. Then he'd hand me the bottle. '*One* gulp,' he'd say. I'd take a gulp. I didn't especially like beer but it was nice, we two men together, to have a beer after work. —

15

Then there were still my big sister and my little one. My big sister was like my mama, fat, and laughed day in, day out. My little sister was small, too small to be a squaw of the Navajo tribe, too small for anything actually.)

'We're going into Mr Kremer's garden,' Mick said when he'd actually drunk his morning milk. 'I'm going to get my feather.'

'Not today,' I said, feeling my heart beat faster. 'I want to go to where they're building the new houses.'

'Why?'

'Or to the gravel quarry. Or to both.'

We crossed the meadows to a building—so far away it was just a distant dot—a building which a few short weeks ago had not yet stood there, which was far from finished. *That* was what a villa was, *that* would be a proper villa! The walls had been built, true, but they were still unplastered. Red bricks with round air holes. The roof wasn't yet tiled. The beams went up into the sky at an angle, and across them, where they met, lay the topping-out beam, the length of the house. Standing on that, from the topping-out ceremony, was a may tree, a fir decorated with coloured ribbons that reminded me of Mick's mother. No glass in the windows. Scaffolding around the house, building rubble and, away from the house, a little toilet hut. A wooden cabin for the workers. Today was Sunday though, so there were no workers and a visit by the architect wasn't expected. We'd never seen the architect, just as we'd never seen Mr Kremer, and like the latter, the architect was the greatest imaginable bogeyman to us.

We ran across the joists on which the parquet floor had still to be laid. On the first floor, especially, running across the room soon tested your courage, the gaps between the beams were so wide that I'd to take huge leaps to make it across the yawning black abyss. Landing, every time, involved struggling to regain your balance, it was best not to stop at all and skip on to the next beam. And repeat this, again and again, till you reached the opposite wall. Richi Wanner had actually once plummeted from the first floor and — without any contact with the beams of the future flooring at ground-floor level — hurtled down into the cellar and landed on a pile of sand. As if nothing had happened, with a crooked smile, he scrambled back up into the daylight. We though — Mick and I — jumped from beam to beam with wonderful certainty, laughing together when we got to the other wall. Then, in the cellar, we filled a bucket with cement. That was stealing and the thrill of the forbidden went through me as I stood beside Mick, watching how he put shovelful after shovelful into the bucket. (He wanted to make a fish pond.) Later still, we ran the few hundred metres over to the gravel quarry that—visible only at the last minute and with no safety fence whatsoever around it—vanished down into the depths behind an embankment of old grass. A very steep, well-nigh vertical wall of white gravel, a twenty- or thirty-metre drop. Below, far below, was the floor of the quarry, full of piles of gravel of different calibres. Rough, medium, fine. Around them, the tracks of lorries that, coming from the other side, could drive into the arena.

Mick was the first to jump down the wall. Gravel travelled with him as he slid—holding his arms out to keep his balance—down into the depths with the grace of a modern-day snowboarder. In no time, he was standing at the bottom and waving at me.

I, too, lunged into the abyss. Unlike Mick, I unleashed a veritable avalanche of gravel in which I was soon helpless as it took me with it. I fought to keep my balance, fought for my life, steadying myself with my arms like Mick had done, not as elegantly though, in undisguised panic, more like. Like Icarus, once half of his feathers had melted. When I reached the bottom, my head, at least, was still above the gravel—but I was up to my chest in the avalanche. 'Mick!' I shouted. 'Mick!' I roared, for I could see the same Mick running off, via the exit the lorries used. He disappeared into the forest. I tried to free my arms—succeeding after, say, ten minutes that seemed like an eternity to me—and set about digging myself out. I didn't have a shovel, I'd my hands. Each time I threw away a handful of gravel, a new handful took its place. I cried for a while. Then I started scooping out gravel again, stubbornly, despairingly, and after another eternity managed to free my right leg from the rotten gravel. Next, I pulled out my left leg. My foot had got caught on something, I heaved and pulled and, finally, my foot shot out. And with it, some white, odd, shapeless thing. With the last of my strength I brought it out into the fresh air. A bone. A large, unthinkably huge bone, clean as a whistle and shining as if it had been washed by twenty million downpours in ten million years. I got the thing up on my shoulder—it was as heavy as a tree trunk— and went back on the same path Mick had taken to the villa being newly built. The same one, my best friend, was sitting on a pile of sand with the bucket of stolen cement between his feet. 'At last,' he said. 'What's that?'

'A bone,' I said. 'I excavated it. From a mammoth, I'd say.'

'Or a *Tyrannosaurus rex*.' Mick weighed the gigantic find in his hands. 'They were able to fly and darkened the sky if they descended on you from a height.' He nodded and gave me the bone back. 'Gravel quarries were their favourite place to live in.'

We ran across the floor beams on the first floor a few more times and climbed up onto the ridge of the roof as the carpenters' ladder was still there, resting against the highest beam. Mick dared first, even he climbing carefully from rung to rung, then it was my turn. From up here I could see really far. On the left, in the distance, our house, Mick's house, Mr Kremer's villa and, yes, the white lady's flat castle that together formed a little village on the plateau, an island of houses among the meadows and fields full of may trees, beyond which—far below—the lights of the distant tiny houses of the town shone. The Rhine, a shining ribbon, disappeared into the horizon that, on the right, was called Germany and on the left, France.

On the other side and much closer was the battery, a bulwark—from the point of view of modern military technology, somewhat laughable—with which the Stadt-Basler once wanted to protect themselves against the furious Land-Basler, and the water tower. The tower—massive—soared upwards. A few townhouses too. Behind them, the blue hills of the Jura. On the road leading to the new villa being built, a few walkers. A woman in a red dress, two men in hats. A dog was frolicking around them and every now and then, one of the men threw a stick that the dog, all excited, chased after.

'The architect!' Mick roared silently at me. 'He's practically in the house already!' He pointed down at the road and hared off—indeed, like that animal—across the beams. I hastened down the rungs of the ladder and could hear, when I reached the floor beams, a voice booming up from the ground floor. I peeked down. In the doorway, where the floorless ground-floor floor began, was the man who had thrown the stick and beside him the other man and the woman in the red dress were squeezing in, trying to have a glance at the room. The dog, a poodle, pushed its head through between the woman's legs. As the men's hats had wide rims, I couldn't see their faces. Just the woman's that was perspiring beneath her platinum-blonde mane. The man I took to be the architect, and who certainly was just that, was explaining something. 'Square metres,' he said. 'Ground plan. Inside insulation. Central heating.' He pointed this way, then that, thankfully not up. I made my way, insofar as I could, with silent jumps to the other side. Where the staircase was. When I reached it though, the other three were already climbing it. I could hear their steps, as if they were three Komturs, and the architect, still talking, sounded like an angel of vengeance from the beyond. What choice did I have, I climbed through the window out onto the scaffolding and jumped. I didn't want to end up, alive, in the hands of the enemy. I'd aimed for the pile of sand and my left foot did indeed land on it but the right landed on a plank with a large nail sticking out. It pierced the rubber sole of my gym shoe and went into my foot. I didn't scream, of course not, a Navajo with an architect on his tail doesn't scream. I pulled the nail from my foot, heaved my prehistoric bone up onto my shoulder and ran, leaving a trail of blood across the meadow. Far ahead of me ran Mick, leaning into the air on one side as he'd the cement bucket in his right hand. I charged into the house, into my mother's arms. She put me in the bath, washed me with a hose from top to bottom — there was a stream of blood at the bottom of the bath and in it, the bone — poured iodine on the wound, then bandaged it expertly. I was now no longer an Indian. I was crying, uncontrollably.

The next few days we did then play in Mr Kremer's garden after all. Mick wanted to, simply, and I'd no arguments with which to persuade him otherwise. I was jumpy, of course, and looked to see if Mr Adamson was around. He and I had a secret, after all, and I couldn't just turn up with Mick at his place. He remained vanished, however. Only on one occasion when, chased by Mick, I ran around the house screaming, did I think I saw him for a second. He peeked his head out from behind the corner of the shed, the one where the garden tools were, the wheelbarrow, the long-since rusty spades and hoes. But perhaps I was mistaken. Mr Adamson's face disappeared as quickly as it had turned up. Like a lamp with a very white light that someone, just for a second, had flicked on and then off again. Mick caught me and threw himself on top of me. We lay there, rolling from side to side, me beneath my friend, both of us gasping and moaning. 'I win!' Mick declared, getting back up.

And so it was several days before I could return to the garden alone. Mick was given detention for several things and then he still had to go to the P. E. for cripples that the doctor sent you to if it looked as though your back was getting crooked or you tended to hang your head in some other way. When I crept through the gap in the boxwood — I dragged, don't ask me why, my bone along with me — Mr Adamson was already on the bench. His legs stretched out before him, his eyes closed, his face turned towards the sun. He was smiling. Maybe he was sleeping and dreaming of the flowers that, really and truly, were running riot all around him. A bee buzzed over him but he didn't wake.

He did raise his head, though, when I ran through the long grass. I climbed onto the bench beside him. He straightened up and again moved away a little.

'Mammoth?' he said, pointing at the bone.

'*Tyrannosaurus rex*. They were able to fly and would swoop down to nab a child and even whole men at times. I excavated it, in the gravel quarry.'

'I used to dig in the past too,' Mr Adamson said. 'For treasure.'

'And did you ever find any?'

'Nothing as old as you have.' Mr Adamson beamed at the dinosaur's bone. 'Shall we play hide and seek? I've not played it for an eternity.'

First, of course, we'd to work out who was to hide first. The rhyme we used was about a cat that had taken a shit and asked how many bits had come out though cats are neither sheep nor goats. Mr Adamson knew the answer. 'Three!' I'd lost. So I put my hands on the wall of Mr Kremer's villa, covered my eyes — which, first, I screwed up tight — counted aloud to fifty, then shouted 'Here I come!' Mr Adamson had disappeared. I took two or three steps away from the wall, far enough to be able to see as far as the garden gate but still close enough to ensure that Mr Adamson couldn't sneak out of a very close hiding place and race up to the wall before me. Because if you play hide and seek properly, the seeker doesn't just have to find the ones hiding, he also has to be first to touch the place where he'd counted to fifty with his eyes shut. Was Mr Adamson lying beneath the boxwood hedge? Was he crouching among the marguerites? Was he on a branch up in the magnolia tree?

It took a long time before I found him in the water barrel from which, somehow, he emerged dry. I was faster at running back to the starting point than him and shouted, relieved, 'One two three for me!'

Now Mr Adamson had to look for me. He, too, stood at the wall, covered his eyes, counted aloud and shouted, 'Here I come!' He found me in no time though I was crouching behind the wheelbarrow, wasn't breathing and had closed my eyes. Then we raced each other a few times, from the garden wall at the rear to the wall at the front and back again. Mr Adamson hotfooted it along at my side — back then, I ran the one hundred metres in seconds, let's say in fourteen-point-eight! — and only fell behind in the final few metres. It was as if he slowed down close to the line. 'Bravo!' he said, when, beaming with pride, I stood at the gate. 'You won!' I was gasping. He didn't seem in any way hot. An ancient old man and as fast as a hare!

'What year is it at the moment?' Mr Adamson said as if he'd heard the question I hadn't even asked—how old he was, actually—and misunderstood it.

'Something starting with nineteen hundred.' I furrowed my brow. 'I'm eight.'

'Nineteen forty-six,' Mr Adamson said and nodded. 'Aha. Already.' He went back to the bench at the wall of the house. I sat down beside him. We remained silent, dangled our legs and watched Mick's cat lying in wait for mice. It sat like a statue in the shade of the magnolia tree, staring at the grass. Every now and then, the tip of its tail twitched. The shadow of the tree that lay across the cat wandered slowly, very gradually, away from it and when the sun suddenly dazzled its eyes, it blinked and raised its head indignantly.

'Now we've become friends, you're giving me an idea,' Mr Adamson said finally, more to his socks than to me. 'We need money.' He looked at me. 'Have you any money?'

'I've got a piggy bank.' He nodded eagerly. 'You put coins in it and then by the time my eighteenth birthday comes along a fortune has been saved.'

'That would be in ten years' time,' Mr Adamson said. 'I was thinking more of something like in five minutes.'

'If you turn the pig upside down and shake it, the coins fall out, just like that. Three minutes is all I need.'

I bolted over to the gap in the hedge, forced myself through it—so quickly that a branch scratched my forehead—ran on the footpath past the bench, along the hedge, across the street without looking, into the house—for a fraction of a second, I saw myself whizzing across the mirror on the wall—up the stairs, into my room. I was gasping. I took the piggy bank down from the shelf, shook as many coins into my cupped hand as would come out—four or five did—and raced all the way back. A total of three minutes later, I was back with Mr Adamson. Four minutes, max. I showed him the money. 'So—what's your idea?'

'Bibi,' Mr Adamson said.

'Who's Bibi?' Blood was running down my forehead over my right eye and I wiped it away with the back of my hand. My hand was now red and clutching the coins.

'My granddaughter. A girl with brown eyes and long hair. She laughs, skips and sings, night and day. The last time I saw her, she was four. We played hide and seek. She was wearing a red-and-white-checked plastic apron and I was wearing this very cardigan and no shoes. I'd taken them off, you see, for Kimmich the shoemaker to mend. I crouched behind a low shelf full of shoes that were already mended, it was hard not to see me, and watched how she nonetheless failed to find me. Yes, and then—' he laughed, a little embarrassed, and raised his shoulders. 'I hope she still lives at the same place. It would be too far on foot for you. You need the money for the tram.'

He jumped up, like a young man, or, rather, more like a keen infantryman in the Napoleonic army, finally able to set out for Russia. 'Let's go!' His eyes twinkled. His cardigan, a grey woollen thing actually, turned into a hardy soldier's uniform and his socks, though they remained socks, became seven-league boots. It was a wonder he wasn't suddenly sporting a moustache and swinging a stick in one hand. Without paying any more attention to me, he set off, at least not straight out through the gate but in the direction of my gap in the hedge. I ran in behind him. I didn't have a stick, true, less still a sabre, but I did at least have my bone. At the top, there was even a round head, something like a knob that felt cool to the touch of the hand that wasn't carrying the tram fare. I swung it like a young miller, setting out into the big world for the first time.

We went down the street that was so empty that we could walk down the middle without encountering a car. Like two giants, a big one and a little one. A father and his son or, rather, a grandfather with his grandson who was giving himself to him with all his heart. I almost reached for his hand. Only my bone prevented me from doing so and the fact that, while walking too, Mr Adamson kept his distance. He knew splendid marching songs though, first one in which a father was walking with his son—a little like us—throughout the many verses and to the bitter end which involved the son, me, despite all his papa's warnings, being sent to the gallows. Next—I knew this one too and crowed along at the top of my voice—it was '*Un kilomètre à pied*' and so on, '*deux kilomètres à pied, trois, quatre, cinq*', till we tired of it. Mr Adamson winked at me like someone planning a good trick grins at his accomplice and I grinned back. An adventure! From the houses—down here, close to the tram stop was where the real town began—came, from a hundred open windows simultaneously, the time signal of the national broadcaster. Three whistle sounds, like those of a tea kettle, the third a semitone higher than the other two. 'It is twelve-thirty. This is the news of the Swiss News Agency.' Mr Adamson stopped and with a sweep of his arm pointed to all the houses surrounding us and said, 'Some things never change in this fleeting world. The sun, the moon and Radio Beromünster.'

The tram came almost immediately. The 16. Green, a dirty dark green. We got into the rear carriage and sat down on the wooden bench. Mr Adamson looked out of the window, of all the windows at the same time, like a boy travelling by tram for the first time and not wanting to miss anything. His head turned back and forth and his eyes shone. In the Wolfsschlucht, where the tram — technically in town, still — travelled for a while between conglomerate rock and black oaks, he even got up and pressed his nose against the glass. Once, when on a bend the tram jerked especially violently, his head even seemed — as if the glass were no obstacle — to float outside, in the fresh air. He pulled it back in — of course, I'd been mistaken — and sat beside me again. The conductor came. 'A half to Hammerstrasse,' Mr Adamson said, to me. I said, 'Hammerstrasse. Half fare, please.' The conductor, a heavy man in a dark uniform, tore a pink ticket from a wad — there were white, yellow and blue tickets too — and, with a considerable puncher, clipped a hole in the route map where he supposed Hammerstrasse to be. I gave him one of my coins. He pushed it into a slit in his machine — it was attached to his belt and looked like a tiny organ with five or six pipes — and with a few quick thumb movements pressed out several smaller coins that, together with my ticket, he put in my hand. 'Change onto the 4 at Barfüsserplatz,' he said, without a word to Mr Adamson.

'Don't you need a ticket?' I asked.

'I'm the conductor,' the conductor said.

'I didn't mean you,' I said to the conductor.

'Who then?' the conductor said.

'Me,' said Mr Adamson.

'Him,' I said, pointing to Mr Adamson. But the conductor continued to look at me and then moved on, shaking his head.

At Tellplatz though, so after only four stops and still far from our destination, Mr Adamson suddenly jumped up and out of the tram that was already about to move off again. I jumped after him. Now the tram did move and I gave my knee such a whack with the dinosaur bone, it ended up bleeding. This blood, too, I wiped away with the back of my hand.

'That's Tellstrasse,' Mr Adamson said. He pointed at it. I nodded, I knew it after all. Right before us was the shoemaker's that had once belonged to Mr Kimmich. At the far end of the street, you could see the masts and overhead wires of the station.

'I thought we were going to Hammerstrasse.'

'Tellstrasse first. That's the correct order.' Mr Adamson craned his neck and set off quickly. He walked past Mr Kimmich's shop window — shoes, and a black plaster boy grinning and offering a tin of shoe polish — without looking at it. 'We'll soon know now whether the house was bombed.'

It hadn't been bombed, Mr Adamson's house, it was destroyed just recently. A crane swung a fat iron ball into the walls and then, with every successful hit, a new piece crashed to the ground. Half the house — the roof and at least one floor — had already gone and the demolition ball was in the process of smashing to pieces the remaining walls on the first floor. As had been the case with the neighbour's house when it was bombed, there was a piece of floor, except there was no lamp on this one but a kitchen stool, painted white. I looked up at it as I'd look at a stage set. When the iron ball prepared to strike again, Mr Adamson ran — without ducking — over to the front door, above which some black wall had remained. The ball was heading straight for his head — I closed my eyes — but he reached the door safely. I reached it just as the metal ball, swinging back, crashed into the masonry above my head. A deafening noise that made me think I'd been hit. My ears were roaring. Rubble and mortar rained down. Air made of plaster that I was eating, rather than breathing. When — fast-as-a-hare Mr Adamson had disappeared long since — I jumped down the cellar steps, bits of stone pursued me; overtook me, even. A block of something hit me in the back so hard I ended up sprawled on the cellar floor. I lay there, moaning, with my arms over my head — stones, lots of them, then suddenly

not any—coughing into the cement of the floor. The bone
was buried beneath me. This is what an air raid had to be
like, the residents in the house next to Mr Adamson must
have run down into the cellar like this. All that was missing
was the phosphor, the firestorm. Again, the demolition ball
crashed into the masonry. The noise was now a bit further
away, at least.

The cellar was pitch dark. Mr Adamson was standing
in a beam of light that, like a spotlight, was lighting him at
a slant through a hole. He'd escaped the rockfall and looked
as if he'd just had a bath. Not a speck of dust on his bald
skull. He was all flustered, though, pointing at the floor
with both hands and calling, 'Help! Come on, help me!'
Part of the floor wasn't cement but wooden. A plank that
was just as grey as its surroundings. Mr Adamson couldn't
lift it, he couldn't even hold a poker that was lying among
a few bits of coal in a recess. He didn't try at all. He must
have had gout, the kind of arthritis that also stopped my
grandad from opening the clamp on the beer bottle with
that karate chop my papa could perform so perfectly.
Granda, like Mr Adamson now, needed a healthy person
to help him. (My papa often told me that—he was the
healthy person and was afraid this story would soon repeat
itself between me and him.) So I took the poker and poked

33

about in the cracks around the plank. Levered up and
down, to and fro. Crunching sounds, scratching sounds,
creaking sounds, and otherwise, nothing doing. I was about
to give up—after, with the last of my strength, attempting
to hit the poker now jammed between the wood and the
cement—when the plank shot up and hit my chin. 'Yes!'
Mr Adamson cheered. 'You managed!'

As I rubbed my chin, I could see a filthy something or
other lying in a hollow scarcely any bigger. Mr Adamson
directed me with the excitement of a grave robber who
finally, after decades of effort, had made it into the inner-
most chamber of the Great Pyramid and was kneeling
before the ancient shrine that contained the riches of the
king of all kings or even the king himself. What I lifted
out, however, wasn't a coffin but a small leather suitcase,
covered in mud, and with a handle that was sticking out
because one end had snapped. 'Quickly!' Mr Adamson
urged. 'It's past my beer time!'

I was on the very bottom step when the ceiling of the
cellar collapsed. The house was giving up. So with the suitcase tight against my chest, I rushed back up to the earth's
surface and out of the front door, the frame of which—
three lonely blocks of stone—was at the top of the staircase.
All the walls had gone. Mr Adamson was just emerging on

the opposite pavement and joined a handful of shameless onlookers who were enjoying the drama of destruction and whose curiosity now turned to me. Two old men with sticks, an old man, a bit younger, with crutches under his arms, and an ancient old guy who used a push trolley made of blue steel tubes to steady himself. His awkward gaze was directed down towards the ground. The collapse of the house he could follow, if at all, only as a shadow play—as Plato had once done. I went up and joined Mr Adamson and turned around.

The frame of the front door was standing like an ancient Greek temple in a cloud of construction dust. The demolition ball crashed into it and these last remaining stones shattered too. 'Boy!' said the crutches-man, standing right behind me. 'What's that you've stolen from the house?' He tapped the case with one of the crutches. His friends shuffled towards me.

'Let's go,' Mr Adamson said. The four old men stuck to our heels, each walking as fast as he could. One of the two with sticks, a scraggy ghost, all skin and bone, had a sprightly stride and I really had to run to avoid his stick. 'Thief! Blackguard! Robber!' The other three were threatening us too, the second stick-man, the one with the crutches and the hunchback with the push trolley who, with his tiny steps, shuffled along at the rear, his squeaky voice moaning at the ground. Soon, Mr Adamson and I had put some good and proper distance between us and them, and by the time we boarded the tram at Tellplatz all four let up on us and went back to the building site.

We changed onto the 4 at Barfüsserplatz. This tram, unlike the 16 a short while before, was pretty full. We couldn't get a seat and Mr Adamson, squeezed into a corner, was trapped by a woman with two big shopping bags and a snotty man wearing a brash cap, pushed back—otherwise it wouldn't have seemed brash—to say kiss-my-arse. He was blowing his cigarette smoke right into Mr Adamson's face. Mr Adamson looked disgusted but didn't say anything. He didn't even blink. I stood there, pressing the case against my chest. It was light, light as a feather.

Hammerstrasse: grey houses built close together, not a tree in sight. A grocer's shop, a tailor's, a shoemaker (called neither Mr Kimmich nor Mr Drzlbrnk), an electrician, a joke shop. Mr Adamson turned into a courtyard, walked diagonally across the yard and up to a door. As we climbed a dark staircase—I now had the case up on one shoulder— he said, 'Ask for Bibi. She lives here with her mama. Don't tell her I'm with you.'

He stopped at a door, pointed with his chin at the bell
and withdrew behind the banister of the stairs leading up
to the next floor. But, if he did that, this Bibi one or her
mama would spot him right away! I rang the bell.

A woman opened the door. Apron, scarf, a cleaning
rag in one hand. If she was the mother, then I'd imagined
her differently. She stared at me as if I was an apparition
from another world, or some monster.

'Bibi,' I said. 'I'm looking for Bibi.'

'There's no Bibi here.'

She closed the door. Through the opal glass I could
see her silhouette moving away. I turned around to Mr
Adamson. His head was peeking over the banister. 'Ask
her where Bibi lives now. Her surname is Huber.' I rang
the bell again.

'Where does Bibi live now?'

'Right, that's enough, you dirty rascal!' This time the
woman slammed the door so intently, the glass in it rattled.

'Her surname's Huber,' I told the opal glass.

Mr Adamson, behind me, was calling something across.
He was agitated, of course he was. 'Try Schneemann' or
something like that. Maybe it was Schniemann he said, or
Schlehmann. I rang the bell again. For a long time, really

insisting. Not a sound in the flat. Mr Adamson was now standing beside me, flaring up like God's avenger angel. 'Schneemann!' he roared. 'Schniemann! Schlihmann!' His roaring achieved nothing either. 'Her name was Huber back in those days,' he told me, much more quietly. 'But perhaps her mama has married the papa in the meantime.' He stared at the door as if he wanted to smash it to pieces with a mighty kick. 'Schliemann!' Then, though, he noticed he'd only socks on his feet and just sighed. He did an about-turn to the right and went down the stairs. I followed him, bent beneath the suitcase on my shoulders. In the courtyard he turned around and looked up to the windows on the first floor. Dusty panes of glass, no shutters. Behind one of the panes, the shadow of the woman's head, spying on us. Mr Adamson turned to face her, stuck his tongue out and shook his fists at her. The woman just carried on staring.

'Bibi's now twelve,' Mr Adamson said with a very different voice, turning to me. 'And really big. Imagine, twelve!'

I tried to imagine a really big twelve-year-old girl, Bibi, but without much success. This Bibi one could get knotted as far as I was concerned. Mr Adamson, though, was just standing there, dreaming away to himself. 'So close,' he mumbled. 'So close!' I was as quiet as a mouse but felt like stroking his hand. Like comforting him. *I* was there after all! I was about to do so when, suddenly forceful again, he raised his head and with one arm signalled a command that seemed to apply to an entire troop. We walked to the tram and travelled back the way we came.

In the garden of Mr Kremer's villa, I was finally able to put the suitcase down. A suitcase *plus* a bone wasn't exactly easy to carry, and without any help from Mr Adamson! I dipped my shirt in the water barrel and wiped the lid of the case clean. I'd nothing better, the case in turn looked like a grave find. On the actually brown—probably—leather were stickers from half a dozen hotels. Bellavista, Splendid or Al Porte Genovese. One sticker, the biggest, was in a script I couldn't read. 'What does that say?' I asked. 'Sintagma Palace, Athinai,' Mr Adamson answered. 'I got around the world in those days.'—On the edges of the lid and the case were two large red-enamel seals. No one could have opened it without breaking the seals. No one had even tried, of that there was no doubt.

In the shed we found a gap in the beams where the case fitted well. It would survive for decades as long as Mr Kremer didn't start digging around in here. I didn't ask Mr Adamson why he didn't open the case. What was in it. Those, I think, would have been the wrong questions. I did, however, say,

'The treasure?' Mr Adamson nodded. I pushed a plank in front of the case and threw all kinds of junk on it.

Mr Adamson headed towards the house. He probably wanted to sit on the bench. I ran after him at any rate and, just as I caught up with him, tripped over a slab in the path and tumbled to the ground. Putting my arms out, I tried— 'Excuse me!'—to use his back for support. But I simply fell right through him. No resistance, at most the feeling that there was some chilly air there. I lay before him on the slab path and, shifting onto my back, looked up at him. He was standing there, grinning like someone you've just caught cheating. 'Oh well,' he said. 'Now you know.'

He took a big step over me. At the wall of the house, he turned around and called back, 'No birds with golden feathers today!' Without stopping, he walked into the wall and vanished. I rubbed my eyes and rushed up to the wall. It was there as it always had been. Solid plasterwork. Not a scratch on it. I tested the mortar, tapping with both hands. Nothing. Nothing unusual. A beetle climbed up between my fingers.

Blindly, screaming perhaps, I took my bone and bolted home where I woke in front of the big mirror in the hall. Where the shirt had been, my skin was pink. As clean as an unweaned piglet. But my arms, my trousers, my legs, my shoes were covered in silt and plaster dust. All over my knees was dried blood, mixed with rubble dust. My head! A mask of dirt and blood. My hair was standing on end like white flames. Only the eyes of the strange monster that I now was were two black circles. No wonder the woman in Bibi's apartment had slammed the door! Behind me, in the reflection, stood my mother whose eyes looked just as horrified.

After that, I was sick, very sick. A meningitis-like reaction, my mother later told me the diagnosis was, verging on meningitis itself. I'd a temperature, way over forty, couldn't bear the slightest light. A thin strip of light beneath the closed venetian blinds, even just the finest chink, and I'd scream with pain. My mother sat by my bed for hours; I was aware of her, and yet not. I was inside a bell where things roared and flickered. It was as if my mother were a shadow. And yet *I* was the one about to become a shadow. I had feverish dreams. In one, the worst, my mama and my papa were both standing, upright, next to each other, in Mick's fish pond—the one we'd made with the stolen cement—in a thick sludge, from which, like two water lilies, their panicked, upturned faces rose. Their mouths open, swallowing the sludge and coughing it up again, then swallowing it once more. They were drowning. Or more like, they were dissolving. I could see them fade away, the sludge was now crystal-clear water, and yet they could barely be seen any more — Papa and Mama. Two shadows, under the water. Then they were gone completely. Had dissolved in Mick's horrible fish water. Instead, Mr Adamson's horrified face, right up against the window. He was calling something but I could only see his mouth, how it was moving. Like that of a fish. — I woke up screaming, imploring my mother who was bending over me not to let me die, not today. 'Because it's Friday!' — It was a Friday, as my mother later confirmed. To this day, I don't quite get the point of my argument. Why shouldn't I die because it was Friday? Incidentally, today *is* a Friday. Friday, 22 May 2032, the day after my ninety-fourth. Two months to the day after Goethe's two-hundredth birthday. Anniversary, I mean, of course, the bicentenary of his death. The fuss they made was incredible, all kinds of memorial events, Sprüngli was even selling lifelike death masks made of white marzipan. — My mother, terribly alarmed, spoke calming words to me. And I did become calmer though my skull was almost exploding. Somehow, at some point, I became well again. The light of the sun first hurt less, then — one clear morning — not at all. I dared to take my first steps. My mother accompanied me and I let her take my hand as I once had as a small child.

One hot afternoon—it was 7 August, I knew and know still because it was *Mick's* birthday—I ventured back into Mr Kremer's garden alone. (Mick, the birthday boy, was doing detention again for a handful of misdemeanours.) I hadn't died! I was well! I forced my way—I'd my bone with me, and the chief's feather in my hair—through the gap between the wall of the white lady's gardens and the boxwood that were so withered, their leaves or needles trickled to the ground as I broke my way through. It was such a glowing-hot day, the meadows were burning in the heat and, on the distant horizon, the forest was smoking.

Mr Adamson was sitting on the bench, just a few steps from the part of the wall he'd vanished into last time. His legs were stretched out in front of him, as before, and he'd closed his eyes. He'd put his head back again too. He was sitting there like someone who'd been there for a long time already and was prepared to wait even longer. When— delighted, and a mite anxious—I stalked through the long grass to join him, though, he opened his eyes and sat up straight. He clapped his hands—without making a sound— and shouted with a kind of glee. Sounded something like an archaic 'Ho-ho!', it did, or an old-fashioned 'Shiver me timbers!' With one hand, he pointed to the bench, like a host offering the guest the best seat. I sat down. Despite a growing love I was feeling for him, I sat at the other end of the bench. Between us, there'd have been space for all of our Navajo tribe. For Mick and all the squaws—my big and little sister. The bone, I placed between us.

'So? Do you know now?' Mr Adamson said.

'No,' I said.

'I'm dead,' Mr Adamson said.

'You're what?'

'I'm dead.'

I stared at him. He didn't look in the least dead, Mr Adamson, except, maybe, that even in this unusually hot summer his face was white, as white as chalk, with bright grey wrinkles, a web resembling a spider's, even if his skull as a whole was more like that of a very big olm. His mouth, his overhanging upper lip, his bulging eyes. The three hairs were still one behind the other like milestones.

'I've never seen a dead person before,' I said.

'Firstly, how do you know?' Mr Adamson smiled. 'Secondly, living people can't see the dead.'

'But I can see you!' I exclaimed.

'There's an exception to every rule.' Now Mr Adamson was laughing. 'That's true for the dead too.—You can see me because I died at the very moment you came into the

world. Precisely at that moment. I'm not saying that year or
day or hour or minute or second. I'm saying moment. A
moment, that's when you take a knife that you can cut time
with, very finely, and you cut a second in two halves, and
the first half into half again, and then you cut each half you
get into half again with your fine-cutting time-knife and
you keep doing that, without stopping, all day long. By then
you'll have a hint of time that's still bigger than a moment,
much bigger, but it will have to do for now to help us reach
an initial understanding. —We, you and I, have replaced
each other on earth. Like in a relay race without a baton. I
am your predecessor. You are my successor. Me, you can
see. All the other dead people, you can't.'

'Are there other dead people around here somewhere?'
I asked a bit louder than I wanted to. I clapped my hands
over my mouth and looked around.

'Just a few. One is standing over there, on the garden
wall, for example.'

I couldn't see anyone. Not a soul. Not on the wall, and
not anywhere else. A dog was sniffing at the bench that the
old women had left meanwhile; but it, in all likelihood,
wasn't dead. The sky was blue, the sun glowing. Not a
single bird dared to fly, it would merely have been roasted,
then would have crashed to the ground. As far as the hedge,

only withered brown grass. The air above the hedge was shimmering. Was that the souls? I shivered, despite the omnipresent furnace.

'And here, in this wall, is the exit from the realm of the dead?' I said, slapping the plaster with one hand.

'Entrance, more like,' Mr Adamson said. 'A side entrance.'

He stretched his legs out again and looked in his pockets for something, his cigar probably—I knew this kind of looking from my father—until he realized those days were gone now. He sighed. 'There are a number of entrances. A few thousand, probably, across the world. I personally only use that one. I knew you'd run into my clutches one day.'

I nodded. My heart was beating. I *had* run into his clutches. It just wasn't clear to me whether this was the most fortunate thing in my life or the most unfortunate.

'Here, at this entrance, there is a rate, at best, of ten dead people per day. Not worth talking about. The really big entrances are in Shanghai, in Calcutta, in New York. Paris! I was in Paris once. There, the entrance was between the tracks at the Denfert-Rochereau metro station. Things were lively there! A few hundred of the living on the platforms, unsuspecting underground passengers, and before, behind, beside and mixed among them were ten times as many dead people. Talk about turmoil! That's why the metro in Paris smells so odd, so unmistakeable. Dead people, in those numbers, smell. You can feel them too. If a dead person walks through a living person, the latter shivers, even in summer, if he's not some lump of wood. — We don't give way to the living. There's no point. Simply right through them, dead straight and without any scruples, it was a strange feeling for me at the beginning too. — I was briefed on how to escort someone in Paris.'

'Escort?'

'The predecessor escorts his successor when the time comes. That's his one and only task. Everyone has just *one* successor, as a rule, and shows that person where to go at the end of *his* life. Task completed, he turns to waste. Isn't allowed back up again.'

'A-ha,' I said.

Mr Adamson wanted to close an immaterial button on his cardigan but it slipped through the hole and the wool. 'At any given moment across the whole globe — and think what a moment is! — three thousand people die. Every moment. Now, now, now. About three thousand always, give or take.' He gave up fumbling with his buttons. 'At the moment when three thousand die, three thousand are also born. Again, give or take, naturally. At the moment of my death, the deviation was a whole three. Three thousand and fifty-eight dead, three thousand and sixty-one new-borns. One of them was you.'

Yes. I could understand that much.

'The predecessors, all of them, try to get close to their successor. It's like an urge. We'd like to protect him but can't. It's a bit like with parents whose children have grown up and no longer need them. Painful, a little bit, and a little bit nice too as you're no longer responsible for *everything*.' He smiled. Probably, he was feeling all these things right at this moment. 'When you were sick, I crept around the house. Didn't like at all what I was seeing through the window.'

'What were you calling?' I said. 'You were calling something, weren't you?'

'Friday,' he said. 'I was shouting, "It's the wrong Friday."'

I was trembling now. 'Have you come to fetch me?' My voice was croaky and a sudden sweat ran into my eyes.

'No,' Mr Adamson said. 'Nothing would be more unpleasant for me.'

I was taking deep breaths. My heart was beating nonetheless, maybe my teeth were chattering.

'Every predecessor, incidentally, looks as he did at the moment of his death.' If the sound he now made was laughter, it was a bitter laugh. 'I learnt how to escort from an old lady in the 16th district, whose neck was like a turkey hen's and who was wearing a see-through nightdress. She was barefoot and had to hide from her successor as he, someone high up in the justice ministry with not long to go before retirement, would certainly have called the police, or the emergency service of the lunatic asylum, if he'd encountered on his doorstep a near-naked old woman who, into the bargain, was wearing around her wrinkly neck a pearl necklace that, if genuine, would've been the envy of Madame de Pompadour.' He now really did laugh. 'When we fetched him—he couldn't see me, the apprentice, of course—he did indeed try, with the last of his strength, to reach for the phone. I've had better luck in that respect. A predecessor in a cardigan and brown socks won't give his successor a fright.' He looked at me with his huge eyes. 'Do I frighten you?'

'No.'

'You see.' He nodded, contentedly. 'I was fetched by someone who died young. From some small town in the

Mexican high country. Her face was smashed to pieces and covered in blood. And she was crying.'

'Why?'

'Exactly. *She* was crying, not me. I was just dying. But she knew this was her last time up here.'

'No,' I said. 'I mean, why was she smashed to pieces and all bloody?'

'My predecessor—whose name was Pilar, incidentally, Pilar della Hazienda del Timór Santo or something like that—was in such a bad way because her father wanted to kiss her. He was an advocate and a person to be respected in the town and loved his daughter. But she didn't love him though love between daughters and fathers was common-place among the Mexican notables. Young ladies of one's own social class were otherwise hard to find. She stepped back, two enraged steps to evade her father's arms, and fell off the balcony, backwards.'

I didn't say anything. Mr Adamson was speaking to his socks now, more than to me. 'Those who aren't allowed back up again,' he mumbled, 'come, in the course of eternity, to resemble each other more and more. Shapeless shadows. Disconsolate, naturally. But the most disconsolate are the new arrivals. These hospital nightshirts that hang down the front of them like green flags, and at the back you can see their poor behinds. — I, now, only miss my shoes. They got left behind on Mr Kimmich's work bench. When Bibi found me, my body that is, I was already on my way to the entrance with the Mexican girl. To this one, incidentally.'

I got it. *That* was why he didn't wear shoes. And that was why Bibi was so important to him.

We remained silent. He, because he was thinking of his Bibi, and I, because she was gradually getting on my nerves. True, I wasn't yet twelve, but I was somebody too!

'Why didn't you simply go to Hammerstrasse?' I said, finally. 'Without me?'

'Because that's impossible.' He blinked, presumably for as long as it took for him to banish the image of Bibi and to see me again. 'Dead people can move around within a radius of one hundred paces from the entrance. Any further, they lose all their strength. Only on their final visit is the radius unlimited.'

'But you *ɗiɗ* go further away!'

'I gambled everything on one card. On you. For, if a living person likes a dead person, if a successor likes his predecessor, if he maybe even likes him a lot, or loves him, then he gives the dead person so much strength that the latter, for as long as this feeling lasts, can walk for miles. You had to like me the whole time, ceaselessly.'

'I did like you,' I said. 'I still do.'

'If a woman,' he said, smiling up at the sky, 'falls in love with her pre-deceased, she can give him so much strength, he becomes skin and bone again. Hand and foot. Flesh. She can touch him. They can even—. You know what I mean.'

'No, I don't,' I said.

'It's terrible, they say,' Mr Adamson said, speaking to his feet again, 'if one day or night, the woman doesn't love the dead man any more. She doesn't know, of course, that he's dead, and that he'll be lost without her love. Mid-embrace, he feels his firmness leaving him, and she can feel it too, comprehends without comprehending—and runs off, screaming.'

'We'll find Bibi,' I said. 'One day, the two of us will.'

He looked at me, sceptically. 'Hope is the last thing to go,' he mumbled. 'If in the middle of Hammerstrasse you'd thought: this tottery old man, why should I want anything to do with this twit, I'd have collapsed feebly on the spot, there and then. Finito. That kind of thing is irreversible, no mercy is shown. You can shout for as long as you want,

"Mr Adamson, what are you doing that for? I didn't mean it like that!" And I'm lying where I'm lying, an invisible pile, a patch of shadow, at best visible to someone who, like you, was born at the moment of my death and just happens to be on a trip to Basel and to be going along, of all streets, Hammerstrasse, and takes this human heap to be a drunk, a victim of drugs. Perhaps he gets a fright when he sees the cars driving right through me and not a single local taking any notice of my tragic situation. That's what would happen. For all time and even longer, I'd lie at my final   resting place. I'd see one car after another driving towards me. It wouldn't hurt. But painless repetition is exhausting too. You know you'll never see anything else ever again.'

'You? What do you mean — me?'

'It's just an expression,' Mr Adamson said. 'I mean me, of course. I'm just trying to explain to you the risk I was taking and why I needed you. It could easily have been the case that you hated me. I got you into danger. If the cellar ceiling collapses on your head, you don't necessarily love the person who tempted you in.'

'I'd no time to feel anything at all,' I said.

'I wouldn't have been able even to ring Bibi's bell. Never mind lift the suitcase. You helped me. Thank you.'

'Don't mention it,' I said.

I felt a new wave of hot lava rising within me. Love. It rose from my stomach and filled my chest and made my head feel so hot, it seemed to be glowing. I probably had a red-hot skull.

It was evening now. The sun, a glowing red ball, was going down behind the forest where the smoke rose in columns that no wind was chasing away. Mr Adamson got up. 'I have to go,' he said.

He raised a hand, turned and walked resolutely towards the wall. From behind, in the evening light, he looked like the salesman in the Just advert, but without a hat, or like someone who will walk for ever and ever. He was glowing red. I don't know what possessed me. I got up, at any rate, got hold of my bone and ran after him. And at the moment when Mr Adamson prepared to walk into the wall, I threw myself into him. Into whatever body he had left, into his silhouette which now enveloped me completely. He felt chilly inside, Mr Adamson, frosty, and I moved at his pace. I was inside him long enough—just a few moments—to pass through the entrance with him.

Immediately, sticky air, actually no air at all, a muggy mucus. No light, a black night. I'd experienced this once before, dreamt it during my illness or earlier still. In another life perhaps. Really clinging this time to my very real bone, I slid down a steep slope of gravel and silt, taking scree with me and hoping, at some point, to find my feet — until the bone got jammed in the slippery rock. I held on to it while, beneath my feet, the stones continued to roll. The bone was bending with my weight but remained wedged. My legs were dangling over an abyss.

Everything was black, no light anywhere. Not a sound, only that of my lungs rattling and the roaring beats of my heart. 'Mr Adamson!' I called up the mountain. 'I'm here!' I could hear nothing, nothing at all. 'Help!' I roared but it was as if I were shouting into cotton wool. No echo, no reverberation, my soundless screams falling to the ground like a gobful of May pits. Whatever: Mr Adamson and the exit could only be above me. So I tried to get onto firm ground and began to crawl up the almost vertical wall of gravel or silt. Blindly. I did manage a metre or two before I slipped and had to be glad that, with my legs apart, I crashed onto the bone that, in my excitement, I'd left where it had stuck. I roared with pain and yet couldn't hear myself. Then I huddled on a narrow ledge that I tested with my hands and feet, and that was barely any broader than my shoe. I whimpered soundlessly. I believe, yes, I'd given up on myself, tentatively perhaps, for at least I remained hooked onto the bone until, after several eternities or perhaps a few minutes, I could hear in this absolute silence something approaching a whisper. It came—curiously!—from within me. Life immediately returned to me. 'Mr Adamson?' I called, I breathed.

'You idiot! You fool!' Mr Adamson's voice was indeed inside me, and very upset. 'That's it! Over! Done! Finito!'

I couldn't see him and felt nothing when I flailed about in the night. It was, maybe, the chilly waft that told me he couldn't be far away.

'Can you climb back to the exit?' he asked after such a long silence I thought he'd never speak to me again. He was now calmer, at least. I reached again for where the voice was, into my ear, but couldn't feel anything now either.

'No,' I roared. My voice, unable to get out, thundered about in my skull.

'Then I'll have to take you to another exit. To a less steep one. My goodness, oh my goodness! Whatever happens, let on you're dead.'

'Like this?'

I let my arms hang listlessly, kept my mouth half open and rolled my eyes until the irises vanished beneath the lids.

Whether I looked at the inside of my skull or out at the world made no difference right now. Maybe Mr Adamson had eyes that could cope with this kind of darkness.

'No.' He could *see* me. 'You're standing right on the path. So let's go.'

I walked forward as best I could. I was groping my way along on what Mr Adamson called a path, on a narrow ledge, a rock ledge that was barely the width of a shoe and patently led along a steep face. Along an abyss. The bone was helping me to stay on the ledge and also helping me balance. And so I groped my way forward, step by step. To my right, the rockface. To my left, a void. Still nothing could be seen of Mr Adamson but, every now and then, I heard his voice. 'If you take a wrong step,' he said inside my ear, 'you can forget your life up there.'

Right away, as if that line from Mr Adamson had been a cue, a loud crash broke the absolute silence, a bang similar to the detonation of a bomb that made me step with one foot out into the abyss, into the void, while the other, for the moment, remained on the path, slipping, fighting for its footing. I held the bone level in both hands, as level as was possible, that is, with the rockface on my right. For a while I floundered backwards and forwards, then I did get a foothold. All the while, until I managed to stand still, this

crashing and banging. It was clear, my steps were causing it.
I waited. Silence, indeed, but a calm that was lying in wait
in the darkness like a predator, waiting for my next move.
When, incredibly cautiously this time, I put some weight on
my foot, I immediately triggered some new droning. A different kind, for this time it sounded as if I were stepping on
microphones that were turned up on full volume. That metal-
lic electrical thundering and whistling you get when a sound
system is distorted. Now I could also hear the gravel trickling,
it also much too loudly, down into the depths. Stones rumbled
down the mountainside — they also sounded amplified. The
mountain face was making noise too. It whistled and
screeched even if, standing still, I merely turned my head.
When I walked, the entire ground beneath me roared. And
I *had* to walk. Mr Adamson, who now sounded differently
too, was urging me on with coarse curses that were coming
from outside again. He outscreamed the roaring. The wailing,
the bangs. 'Shift yourself, you stupid ass!' 'Will it be any
time soon, you ape?' 'Do you want to take root or what,
scaredy-cat?' Things like that. My ears were hurting, my
brain hammering. It was still pitch dark though and, step by
step, and ignoring Mr Adamson's nagging, I groped my way
along the wall of the netherworld, leaning my hands on it
for support and poking with the bone for firm ground. If a

stone were to loosen! I was constantly causing deafening noise I could neither avoid nor bear. What if *they* heard me? What if they'd seen through me long since? If they finished me off by electrocuting me? — And yet the biggest danger remained that I might fall. How often was I about to step out into emptiness, only to notice — just in time — a bend in the path!

Suddenly, I was standing in the light. With a single step I moved out of the blackness and found myself in a dazzlingly bright glowiness that, nonetheless, was colourless or, at best, grey. Behind me, the darkness remained like a wall. Mr Adamson was waiting a dozen metres ahead of me and waving. The light had no warmth whatsoever, was so inhospitable that I might have fled back to the protective blackness. At least I could now see the path before me. Still the width of a shoe, it indeed led along a steep wall that vanished deep into a bottomless abyss, making me think of the quarry of yore where the bone came from. And sure enough, here and there, remains poked out of the rubble. Perhaps what was left of people like me, of strays who'd wanted to save themselves and, falling, had been swallowed up by the silt. I stood my bone against one poking out by the side of the path — and it was identical. I even tried to jog it but it stood firm.

From the deepest depth—as far as the human eye could see and almost vertically beneath me—an at times green and at times reddish light source, glowing now more strongly, now more weakly, like a pulse, glimmered up at me. The heart of eternity.—Above me, when finally I, for once, could see upwards, the wall climbed just as steeply but soon hit the sky, more likely the ceiling, of course, the earth's lid. I was seeing the surface of the earth from below. Everything was dark, in twilight, the light sources barely reached up that far. The dark cupola so close, I felt I'd to duck.

The path was like one of those in the Andes or the Cordilleras which, if your plane smashes into a mountain and you're the only survivor, promise you—as they wind their way around one ridge after another—that you'll arrive somewhere and be rescued, only then—after marching for ten hours—to end up in a field of scree, so narrow now, you can hardly turn to go back the way you came and try the other direction. Here, however, I had my Mr Adamson who now looked like an enemy, fluttered way ahead on the path, came back again, whizzed off into the distance again and made impatient gestures at me. I stumbled along as fast as I could, slipping once or twice. The bone saved me.

Only once I'd taken a few dozen steps in the brightness did I notice that the roaring and crashing noises had stopped. That the sounds around me were now different. They were now rising from far below, from those unfathomable depths. Sounds that made my blood run cold. These were *their* sounds, my fear told me. The abyss was thundering, still distant, but getting ever closer. Within the deafening noise from far below there was also, quite distinct, a gurgling, a bubbling, crescendoing every now and then to a rhythm that knew no rules, it seemed. Screams. Pillars of screams. Heart-rending moans. To sigh in even greater despair was impossible. Seemed impossible to me. For, immediately after them, I heard a wail that was even more interminable. Then another, and another. It was absolute pain I was hearing, but an even more radical form instantly followed. Then another, and another. A thousand cries of pain, all distant still. With individual cries soon coming closer, however, and finally merely a stone's throw away. But who would be able to say, down here, how far a stone could be thrown. All pain, even the most extreme, was exceeded by an even more ultimate form. The misery was boundless.

True, I was high above the howling. Still close to the roof of the netherworld. But more and more screams were being aimed at me, as if—like tentacles, reaching for me—

they knew where I was walking; the screams got louder and then loud, droning directly beneath me and touching my feet, then finally sank back. Then, once, a piercing screech, flickering up at me like lightning, combined with such a loud roar striking so close in front of me that I jumped up the mountainside. I slipped back, of course, and crouched with grazed knees on the gravel ledge. I was gasping. Mr Adamson had become a dot on the horizon, unaware of the problems I was having. He wasn't helping me, at any rate, though I needed help like never before in my life.

I was now moaning uninhibitedly — who cared if someone heard me and found me and destroyed me. My sighs were the echoes of the sounds from down below though mine didn't — not by a long chalk — sound so terrible. I was still far from being *as* sore as those moaning down there. That said, I was trembling and quaking and would certainly have jumped, voluntarily, into the abyss had I not had the bone in my hands. Even with its help, it was more difficult to put one foot in front of the other than to take the more radical step. Jumping would have been easy to do. That I could sense. That I could feel. That I mustn't allow. Jumping without thinking was what was required! I'd then have crashed down, head first and with my arms flailing, screaming or entirely silent — how can you know in advance? There'd have been no going back, at any rate. I'd have been released from all this.

Then a stormy gust, or an electrical discharge perhaps, did indeed sweep me out into the abyss. The initial fright was so great, I stopped breathing and my heart was no longer beating. Rigid, I was flying, in cold horror, my feet motionless in the void. It was a long time before the scream that had got caught in my throat did then find its way out. Ahhh! I flailed with my arms and kicked with my legs. The bone had slipped out of my hand. I'd lost any foothold and yet wasn't crashing like a stone into the depths. I was the plaything of unknown elements, carried this way and that by a storm I couldn't feel. Up and down again. I was breathing again now, my heart was racing. I flapped my arms, like a bird, trying to determine the direction I flew in. In vain. At times, for a matter of seconds, I crashed down into the depths—as if free fall had kicked in after all. Head first, somersaulting. Then I'd float up again, like a feather on an air column. My blood was circulating at an ever-faster rate. I could feel it foaming, like the water of a dam bursting or, more like, a volcano erupting—for as it circulated my blood got hotter and hotter, so boiling hot, in the end, that my brain burned and my heart glowed. The heat swamped me from within. It was fear, this heat, and became a panic that swept away with it any fortifications, floodgates and barriers I may have erected inside in the course of the years. At the age of eight, many a dyke is still weak. Some do hold, though. None, however, withstood this tidal wave of horror. I screamed. I'd never screamed like this.

I wished I were blind and yet tumbled with my eyes wide open down through this almighty abyss. I *did* see things but it wasn't that clearly defined recognition of things, in keeping with clear rules by which a tree is a tree, unmistakeably so, even if I'd never seen one like that before. Nothing here was delimited, everything emerged from everything else and, like me, was crashing down or floating up. Where did one thing end and the next begin? Cloud formations, shifting, changing, grimaces perhaps, enormous or tiny, far off or right in front of me — how was I to make things out? (Add to that the now very loud howling or roaring bursting my eardrums. And I was screaming too.)

This was the world Mr Adamson came from. It had to be, for sure. It could also be, though, that I'd fallen deep into myself. This, I reckoned, was what inside me looked like too. Back then, back then certainly. That black core I'd never looked into, and I sensed the existence of only because, from time to time, and beneath the brightest sun, nightmare flashes would frighten me. Just as Mr Adamson had suddenly stood before me.

Had I somehow ended up in the force field of that black hole inside me that sucked in and preserved everything I experienced? The force field of that secret reservoir that contains everything, yet hardly ever releases anything? That was what it was, that could be what it was: I was now within, inside me, and could see! but could no longer — that was the price to be paid for my audacity — escape being swallowed up by my own reservoir. I'd stumbled into my own memory. And was now trapped there for ever.

Images flashed up, briefly enough — true — for me to know that I knew that was the solution. The images, though, blurred before I could grasp them. — And so, ruffled, I flew through my truth. But the apparitions were evaporating so quickly that, while I stared in frightened recognition of one thing, the next would already be rushing in on me and crowding out the first. Then the next would arrive, and the next. All kinds of apparitions wildly chasing one another. Me, swamped with sweat and as wide awake as you can be when your eyes settle on something bringing death in its wake. Sometimes you could almost see that *something* was happening. But what?

Had I lost my mind? What was I now walking in? Was I wading through something like wet moss? In a morass of blood? Were others walking here too? Was I dead? Was part of the ugly side of escorting the fact that Mr Adamson —Was he walking beside me? Was he inside me? Was I walking inside him?—let me think I could get back out? What was it that was always urging me forward? Blood, didn't it smell of blood here! This immeasurable red sea, was that the blood of all those who'd died till date? Could I see them, transparent, in shadow? These endlessly sad faces I was urged past, and through which I walked—did I know them? Had I seen them before, these eyes that didn't beg, that held no hope?

Were the souls around me now getting restless? Because of me, even? Were they beginning to sway to and fro? Oh! Oh! They were looking at nothing in particular—there was no clear object of attention yet—but in such a hostile way! Malicious way! Could I really hear Mr Adamson thinking, 'Faster, man!' 'Pull yourself together!' Yes, but how? Was I really walking like a Groucho Marx trying to escape, taking such huge steps, they could pass as having no design? Was I sweeping through the ranks of the dead so quickly that suspicion was always arising behind me while before me stood another few million clueless souls? Were the mouths of individual souls, right behind me and here and there before me, now gaping open? Showing shiny sharp teeth? And, with their big eyes, were they beginning to look for their target? Me?

Was I singing to save myself? And was Mr Adamson running now too, like me, leaning his upper body far forward and taking long steps? Was he singing too? Were the dead all beginning to comprehend *together*? Was outrage, multiplied by millions, setting in as far as the horizon? A storm of wailing? And could it be that my singing was saving me? These cheeps? Because, when I produced these few puny notes, the dead closest to me, all howling now like the hurricane to end all hurricanes, hesitated — astounded — for a moment to perform that fatal bite and I, meanwhile, had been able to flee again, beyond their biting range, etcetera? Was the bone helping me? How come it was back in my hands? Ah, the dead, the dead didn't want to let me live. I could feel, as I fell, that I couldn't resist them. I gave up. 'If the dead want you,' was my final thought, 'they'll get you.'

As if, crashing to the ground, I'd tumbled through a wall, I could see clearly again. I was lying on stones, on a warm stone slab. A sun, very low in the sky, was dazzling me just as it had done when I'd set off. Was I back in Mr Kremer's garden? I breathed in and out. The air was magnificent. I gave a loud groan. The colours! The light! The sun was so dazzling, I could barely see Mr Adamson though he was standing right over me and wiping the sweat from his brow. There wasn't any sweat, and no brow that he could have touched either, but Mr Adamson, too, was all over the place.

'Phew!' he said.

'You can say that again!' I answered. I closed my eyes and immediately fell into a deep sleep.

When I woke again, the sun was still in the same place. So, though completely exhausted, I'd nodded off for just a few seconds, not longer! The equivalent of three or four deep breaths, it seemed. Mr Adamson was still next to me but no longer standing and wiping away imaginary sweat. Rather, he was squatting on a stone not far from me, and constantly looking—jerking his head, rooster-like—before, behind and above him. I picked myself up, stretched my arms, yawned and smiled at him. I felt good, much better than just a few moments before.

'The sun is still where it was in Mr Kremer's garden,' I said.

'Shush!' Mr Adamson hissed, still looking here and there, and not looking at me. He whispered from a mouth, the lips of which were closed tight and barely moved. 'We're not as alone as you think.' I looked around—not a soul far and wide—and felt a chilly blast of air pass me. I began to shiver and looked at Mr Adamson.

'Get you!' I whispered.

'And don't look at me when you're speaking to me!' *He* wasn't looking at me.

'No time at all has passed!' I said as quietly as he'd spoken, looking at a yellow stone lying between my feet. 'And I'm wide awake and fresh as a daisy!'

'You slept for a night and a day,' Mr Adamson growled through rigid lips. 'Twenty-four hours. And I dare not estimate how much time we frittered away down below. A minute, maybe. But it could also have been a century.'

'A century?' I screamed, I whispered.

'Or a millenium.'

The sun was no longer glaring as much as a moment before—after all the netherworld twilight I'd become light-sensitive—and I began to recognize the contours of a landscape around me. I was sitting at the top of a mountain or, rather, a hill, surrounded by stones glowing in the sun. Ruins consisting of gigantic building blocks. Diagonally below me, a gate on which two mythical creatures hewn in stone kept watch. Further down was a plain, bathed in a red sunset. Across the plain, in a regular pattern, stood individual trees. Olives, I realized immediately, olive trees, though I'd never seen an olive tree before. Or even eaten an olive. 1946! Here and there were houses with flat roofs. A bit farther on, a village that looked as if God, with a very large broom, had swept together a few dozen of these house-shaped dice. I'd become so accustomed to the light of the world of the living meanwhile, I could even discern a farmer driving a tiny donkey. On the horizon shone a strip of light that was perhaps a sea. Behind me, when I turned around, purple mountains. Now I did look at Mr Adamson as if to ask.

'The Mycenae,' he mumbled.

'A-ha.' I'd no idea what he was talking about.

'Greece. There's no other exit that's in any way flat. Entrance, I mean. The most difficult part is now behind you. I now just have to ship you home.'

'Then let's go.'

I lifted the bone and took a first step. Mr Adamson, though, remained seated and was looking around as nervously as before. You would have thought he'd jaws of stone as he growled, 'Can you see that gate down there?' A narrow, steep path led the way via scree slopes, the remains of walls and archaically crooked steps down to the city gate, guarded by the two stone monsters and glowing in the last of the sunlight. 'That's where we'll meet. Once it's dark and we're out of the city, we'll be on the safe side of life.'

I set off without looking at him again. The bone I used as a mountain stick and so I slid only once, and for a few metres, as I went down the scree. Further down, there was even a proper path, the width of a foot, but safe. The sun was so low, it was dazzling me. A few more jumps over columns, stone blocks and walls, and I was standing at the gate above which, invisible to me now, the watchdog creatures were lying in wait. Ahead of me, along a wall of stone blocks as high as a house, a road branched off, downwards. A path made of ancient marble. The stones were all still red in the light of the sun that was sinking beneath the horizon.

Mr Adamson didn't turn up until the sun had completely gone and the sky above it was no longer burning purple. In its place, an almost-full moon was climbing from the horizon. The city gate became a black hole—where I was concealed— and the plain was soon a lake, without any contours, where two or three lights shone. Mr Adamson suddenly stood before me. Through him shone the Ursa Major.

'At last,' I whispered. 'Papa can be quite angry if I come home late.'

'Down here, you don't have to whisper,' he said, with his voice from before. 'We're far enough away from the entrance. And aren't in a hurry any more.'

'But Papa!' I said. 'And Mama!'

'They'll be hellishly annoyed now.' Mr Adamson, he too in the shadow of the gate, spread out his arms. 'In the best-case scenario. In the worst case, they've been dead for a hundred years. Or ten thousand.'

I look at him, appalled. 'So what are we waiting for?' I said, shouting so loudly that Mr Adamson now did raise his finger to his mouth though we were beyond the orbit of the dead by now.

'I'll take you to the police station in the village down there.' A generous sweep of his arm took in the whole plain. 'The policemen there are specialists for your kind of case.'

'What kind of case am I?'

By now he was peering out of the black shadow concealing us and back into the ruins of the antique city towering above us. Suddenly cheerful, he pointed up at the stones. 'That there must be Clytemnestra's tomb.'

'Whose?'

'Have you not heard of Clytemnestra?'

I shook my head.

'Agamemnon?'

'No.'

'Aegisthus? Menelaus? Helen? Paris?'

I held my hands up.

'Schools aren't what they used to be.' He laughed. 'Clytemnestra, she was the queen of all this. I found her tomb. Yes, yes. I did. Together with Schliemann. Heinrich Schliemann. I used to tell the story often, in the past.'

I looked at him with big eyes he couldn't see as we were still beneath the lightless city gate. We were silent for a while.

'Do you not believe me?' he said.

'No, I do. I believe everything you say.' I scratched my forehead. 'Schlihmann. *That's* a name I've heard before.'

'Schliemann is world famous. He excavated Troy.'

'Was that also with you?'

'No, no. Mycenae was later, 1876.'

'1876?! Were you already alive then?' I exclaimed.

'I was *still* alive, young man. Let's go.' He stepped out into the bright moonlight—with me beside him—but immediately stopped again.

'Look. The Lion Gate.' He pointed up. 'Had vanished up to its paws in rubble. A hellish job, I tell you.'

'Are those supposed to be lions?' I laughed. 'Dogs is what they are. Ugly dogs.'

The moon was now high above us. Around us were shadows, the shapes of monsters, of a thousand monsters ossified as they pounced. An animal was rustling in the withered bushes, a hyena maybe, or a mountain lion. The crickets had stopped chirping. In the distance, far distance, a dog was barking. Mr Adamson seemed not to be afraid, not in the least. But I'd have been the same in his position.

'Schlihmann, Schlihmann,' I said as we walked along, side by side. 'Someone mentioned him just recently.'

'Was a dream of mine to be here. With Schliemann.' Mr Adamson was one of those—old men they are, as a rule—who stop when they want to say something. And so Mr Adamson stood still again. 'Here, where it is bright. Here, where it is hot. I'm from Sweden, you see, in case you haven't noticed. At the Arctic Circle, it's eternal night for half your life. And all your life, it's icy cold.'

'A Swede!' I exclaimed, imitating his accent, this singsong of dark vowels. 'And there was me thinking that's how the dead speak.'

'Doesn't matter how I came to be here.' Mr Adamson didn't respond to my little bit of cheek. 'I've different versions of that story. What I told Bibi was: I came to Mycenae because a man by the name of Panagiotis Stamatakis took me with him. Working in the ministry of internal affairs, he was, and tasked with supporting Schliemann. Nominally. In reality, he was to keep a sharp eye on him during the excavation as Schliemann, like the blackbird, had a reputation for stealing. The tendency to do so, too. In Troy, he'd already nicked everything that wasn't screwed down.'

We were standing, in the bright moonlight, at the staggeringly high outer wall of Mycenae. My shadow stood out as a black silhouette on it. It was the only shadow. Mr Adamson didn't cast one. I knew why, yet got a terrible fright when I noticed. Not bothering about Mr Adamson, I ran downhill. He soon caught up with me, though, immediately came to a halt again and spoke to me so heatedly that you'd have thought the story was burning inside him.

'When we arrived up there, we met a Schliemann who was as euphoric as he was exasperated. Euphoric because he was discovering one royal tomb after another, and exasperated because a sharp wind was blowing day and night, an eternal storm that was blowing sand into his and all the others' eyes. After half an hour, you looked like a shifting sand dune. Everyone in Mycenae looked identical, they were powdered beings, digging up the earth with picks and shovels. They all coughed and sneezed so much, we'd been able to hear them at the foot of the citadel already, just before we ourselves were exposed to the wind and also started sneezing and coughing. Whenever I told Bibi the story, we howled, at this part, like the wind—woo! woo!—and then sneezed and coughed. I would laugh and Bibi cheered.'

'Bibi,' I said. 'Yes.'

He stepped closer to me and I was afraid for a moment that he, in the way that old men who stop to speak do, would also put his arm around me. But he didn't. He spoke his story into my ear without me feeling or even smelling his breath.

'Schliemann saw through Stamatakis' part in all this right away and, almost instantly, the two couldn't stand each other. I didn't find Schliemann especially likeable either. He was quite a son of a bitch, to tell the truth. He had ruthless energy, was up at five in the morning and out after stones. All he talked about was stones. He bossed me around too though I was answerable to Panagiotis Stamatakis. I was his assistant, you see, even if it was unclear why he needed an assistant. Soon, I was digging like a man possessed too, with Schliemann on my back —who had a talent for always turning up if I sat down on a stone to rest for a second. Or if I'd found something terrific. A sherd, a still-perfect sacrificial vessel even. He'd snatch it from my hands and show everyone what *he* had found and then made me dig elsewhere, some-where where two metres of dirt had to be removed first before it got interesting again.'

'Then *you* found the treasure!' I didn't ask. I made the observation. And took the opportunity to move forward a few steps. The hyena that was maybe a mountain lion had come closer; not far from me, at any rate, I could see a shadow moving. Silence, deep silence, apart from the fact a wind was now, indeed, blowing and causing the thickets to rustle. A chilly wind —was how it felt. Probably though, I was shivering because Mr Adamson, unlike before, was no longer taking care to maintain proper distance.

'Yes,' said Mr Adamson, still close to me. 'No.' I'd forgotten what the question he was answering was. 'Sophia found the treasure and gave it to me as a farewell present.'

Now I remembered what the question was. 'Sophia?' I said.

'Schliemann's wife. I hadn't noticed her at all at first as she was just as filthy as all the others. For more than a week, I thought she was a man and my attention was drawn to her because her spade seemed to detect hidden treasures like a divining rod does water. She would walk over the grass on the surface, say 'There!' and then dig. She was very different from her husband who was like a steam hammer and, in Troy already, would have preferred to blast the castle walls away to get down to the deepest levels. Sophia discovered Clytemnestra's tomb. The treasure in it. A headband dripping with gold, something like golden braids, a necklace made of a hundred gold links. She wanted to hear that a hundred times, Bibi! She loved fairy tales with princesses who have gold and glitter.'

'Squaws,' I said. 'An Indian of the Navajo tribe won't be impressed with that kind of thing. Don't even try.' I tried again to move on a few steps and got as far as the next bend.

'On one occasion,' Mr Adamson said when he'd caught up with me and put on his brake again, 'Sophia wore the jewellery for me. The jewellery was *all* she was wearing.'

'How come?' Now I stood stock-still. Perhaps the nights were so hot back then, she couldn't bear any clothes.

'Because, she was twenty-four. I was barely a year younger! But her husband was fifty-four and spoke about nothing but Homer and the Atridae. To her too. And in ancient Greek! He didn't see, not any more perhaps, how beautiful she was. I told her once when we were shovelling alongside each other and she blushed so much, the sand on her cheeks turned white. You know, don't you, how children come about?'

'Naturally,' I said and then choked. I coughed so much, my head seemed about to explode. When I got my breath back, I added, 'But of course.'

'How?'

'The father,' I said, 'buys some seed and puts it into the mother and then the child grows in her stomach.'

'Exactly.' Mr Adamson smiled. 'I didn't even have to buy the seed. I'd some on me the whole time, a whole sackful.' He suddenly started to giggle. I stared at him, not getting what had made him laugh. He was a silly person, a dead silly person. But his giggles were so infectious, I started laughing too and in the end was roaring louder than he was. I could hardly breathe for laughing. Now Mr Adamson was back to being serious and looking at me.

'One evening, I put the seed into Sophia,' he continued. 'In there, behind the huge wall, when her husband had gone to Athens with Panagiotis Stamatakis and the workers in the village were celebrating the feast of St Christopher. Sophia enjoyed it, like salvation it was for her, and I, too, was completely beside myself. The jewellery was tinkling and jangling as we rolled from side to side in the stubble field. This part of the story, I've never told Bibi. I can tell you because you're much bigger.'

I nodded. I was eight, and this Bibi one had been almost a baby still when Mr Adamson died.

'When the workers returned, we were still behind the wall. But they were all too merry to notice. Plus, it was the night of the new moon. Schliemann and Stamakatis returned only four days later. Four nights later. They were at loggerheads—so much so, Schliemann had his official supervisor airbrushed out of the legendary photo of the excavation team. Same thing happened to me, oddly. Where we stood—right beside Schliemann—there's now a gap. The others are looking into the camera with the seriousness that was par for the course when you were photographed back in those days. Right at the edge is Sophia, the only person not looking at the photographer. She's looking at me though I've vanished from the picture.'

The moon above the ruins had disappeared; its light, though, was still bathing the plain before us in brightness. The wall had turned black and Mr Adamson, now in the dark, looked like a king from the olden times in silhouette or, even more, my Manitou who, the only one not asleep, would oversee his kingdom by night too and ensure everything was as he'd envisaged.

'Sophia had a child. A son. Schliemann called him Agamemnon. Wouldn't settle for any less though Sophia would've preferred to call him Costas. He's *my* son.'

'Your son?' I exclaimed.

'I'd have called him Knut. We've all been called Knut for generations now. Knut Adamson. Sounds better than Agamemnon Schliemann, doesn't it! But that's how things go sometimes.'

'Now I remember!' I threw my arms up. 'Bibi! That's where I heard the name before.'

'Agamemnon was her father. She called him Paps and me, Uncle Knut. I tracked her down in Basel, in Hammerstrasse. That I was her grandfather, I didn't ever tell her. Her mama was too proud of old Schliemann, prouder than of her child's father. For Agamemnon, the question didn't even arise. He'd no doubts, that boy, and nor did he look after his child or her mother. Just like his old man in that respect.'

'Good story,' I said.

'Hard to believe, eh?' He was beaming.

The hoot of an owl, hidden somewhere in the wall, and from high up it sounded as if now scared animals were fighting. Bats. Mr Adamson raised his head and sniffed the air. 'Enough dawdling!' he said. 'Time to go to the police!'

Now he was sweeping ahead of me so quickly, I could barely keep up. I tripped over stones and steps I couldn't see in the dark. Down on the plain it was better. The path, straight as a poker and much broader, and far ahead, like a guiding star, a single light announcing the village. Olive trees growing everywhere, their leaves shining in the moonlight. The ground black, half earth, half scree. On one occasion, seven or nine chunky shadows moaning beneath the trees— sheep whose sleep we'd disturbed. The air was hot. The moon had passed its zenith and, still bright, was slowly sinking towards a dark black mountain range to my right.

The police station was the first house in the village. A white cube, for sure, with, no doubt, a bright blue door that, now at night, was black. Two blank windows. Shutters that were bright blue, surely, too. Two bicycles, up against the plaster of the wall. In the dark, they looked like two skinny animals. No light above the door, no neon sign. Everyone knew here where law and order hid away. Mr Adamson turned to me. 'Don't forget, the police can neither see nor hear me. When we go in, an eight-year-old boy—in their eyes—will be crossing the threshold. All alone. You'll be able to speak some Greek because I'll say things for you to repeat. Let's see if they can help you.'

I pushed the door open. A room that was so dark, I could see absolutely nothing at first and then, gradually, two shadows sitting motionless at a long table. A bare bulb dangled from a wire above them. I blinked. Indeed, two policemen in bright shirts, whose upturned hats lay like soup bowls on the table in front of them, the surface of which many generations of policemen had covered with ink stains and cigarette burns. I stood where I was. 'Say Kaliméra!' Mr Adamson said, behind me. 'Kaliméra!' I said and approached the table. The bone, I was holding in my left hand, like a rifle at the ready. 'Ναι?' one of the officers said, the elder of the two, and certainly in charge here. He'd a bushy moustache, huge eyebrows and skin like a well-used suitcase. His puzzled eyes went back and forth between the bone and my face. Both hands, paws, more like, were on the table, on either side of his cap. His colleague was sitting in the exact same position and now also said, 'Ναι?' He didn't have a moustache, perhaps wasn't able to grow one yet, and his voice squeaked. In his left hand he'd some kind of rosary with yellow beads that his fingers were constantly pushing along the string, so expertly and self-evidently that the fingers of his other hand were able, simultaneously, to tap out a drum roll on the table until the old officer, his father perhaps, lightning fast, and like a cobra striking, rapped him across the fingers with a ruler.

Behind him, on the back wall—I was getting used to the dim light of the bulb—hung a tear-off calendar. It was showing the date as 7 August. The 7th of August! Yesterday, at home, had been the 7th of August too! Though I'd slept for a night and a day, we'd gained a day! My parents wouldn't even be missing me yet! I pointed, for Mr Adamson, at my discovery. Both officers turned and looked at the calendar.

Mr Adamson nodded, three times, vigorously. He was suddenly truly agitated. 'Ask him what year it is. Pió étos échume?'

'Pió étos échume?'

'Χίλια εννιακόσια σαράντα έξι,' said the officer with
the bushy moustache. He raised his eyebrows, making them
touch the hair on his head. His eyes were suspicious round
plates. I couldn't understand a syllable of what he said.

'1946!' Mr Adamson exclaimed. 'Jeepers creepers! Are
you in luck! That's the first time I've known time to go
backwards.'

But now the young policeman stood up, went over to
the calendar and tore the top sheet off. Now, the calendar
showed the date as 8 August. The policeman sat down
again and once more began to busy his left hand with the
toy rosary. The fingers of his right hand were on the table
beside his cap and every now and again twitched nervously.
The old officer had his eye on them and seemed prepared
to give them another whack.

'There we go,' Mr Adamson said. 'We're still very much
on schedule. — Tell them that you've got lost. Échasa to
dhrómo.'

'Échasa to dhrómo,' I said to the old policeman. He
looked more trustworthy to me than his colleague who now
had his mouth open and was panting like a whelp.

'A!' said the paternal policeman, and the policeboy yelped, 'A!'

'A-ha,' Mr Adamson said. 'They're saying: A-ha. Say that your mama and papa are missing you. I mamá mu ke o babás mu me apositún ke dhen xéro to dhrómo na jiriso spiti mu.'

'I mamá mu ke o babás mu me apositún ke dhen xéro to dhrómo na jiriso spiti mu.' I looked at Mr Adamson, who nodded.

'Γιατί έχεις αίμα στα παπούτσια?' the older policeman said, pointing at my shoes. The young policeman even got up, came around the table and bent down to look at my feet. I too looked down, without having understood the question. 'How come you've blood on your shoes?' Mr Adamson sighed. 'Tell them it's raspberry syrup. Maybe they'll believe you. Ine sirópi apó wa-tómura.'

'Ine sirópi apó wa-tómura,' I said.

'A!' The old policeman swayed his head thoughtfully while the young one echoed, 'A!' Both looked at me, for a long time and in silence, as if they'd to work out for themselves: was I some supernatural apparition or an ordinary little rogue. A murderer even.

'Και πού μένεις;' the paternal policeman asked me finally, and I told him, with Mr Adamson always helping with the translation, where I lived. Street, house number. This went back and forth for quite a while, slowly, doggedly and with never-ending gaps as the officers seemed to have all the time in heaven and Mr Adamson didn't always find the correct Greek word instantly. He'd already been away from Athens for a few years and I, no doubt, was the first lost child whose parents lived at the other end of the world as we know it.

'21-1-15!' I crowed, suddenly inspired. I even knew our phone number!

'21-1-15,' Mr Adamson said, in Greek.

'21-1-15,' I said, in Greek.

'21-1-15?' the elderly policeman asked, in Greek.

'Plus the code for Basel,' Mr Adamson said. For code, he said *Κωδhικός*.

'Basel,' I confirmed.

'Basel?' the policeman said, biting his moustache. 'Μακεδονία;'

'No. Not Macedonia,' Mr Adamson said. 'Switzerland.'

'Switzerland,' I said.

'Switzerland?' the officer asked, looking at his colleague who tapped the forefinger of his drum hand against his forehead.

'Will you just call, you slowcoach!' Mr Adamson—suddenly very loudly—roared. 'See to it that this little one gets home to his papa and mama.'

'I couldn't put it any better myself,' I said.

'Κοίτα με όταν μου μιλάς!' the old policeman said.

'He says to look at him when you're speaking to him,' Mr Adamson said, now more quietly again. 'Look at him when you're speaking to me.'

'I'm not speaking to you, you squib!' I roared, looking at the old policeman. 'I'm speaking to Mr Adamson. *Now*, I'm speaking to you!' I pointed at the antediluvian telephone. 'Phone! Phone! Call them!' I did a mime, telling them to dial the number. 'Capito?'

Strangely, the paternal officer seemed to understand. He raised his shoulders, said something like 'yes, yes'— 'Ναι ναι'—lifted the receiver of his phone and dialled. That said, it wasn't the number I'd given him and the person at the other end certainly wasn't my papa. My mama, even. He was making odd sounds, Greek ones probably, at a colleague somewhere far away, in Athens presumably, at someone of a higher rank at any rate as again and again, he nodded with obsequious zeal and soon even stood up. From the receiver I could hear what sounded like hellish hissing. He put a hand over the mouthpiece and whispered something to his colleague. 'Ο χερ Κρέμερ!'

'Oh dear God,' Mr Adamson mumbled. 'The top man himself.' He'd turned pale, as white as chalk, though dead people always look the same, white or, if they died of a stroke, bright red.

When their conversation was over, the old policeman barked a snappy goodbye into the earpiece and clicked his heels. He was in his bare feet. The lad remained seated, true, but he'd put his cap on and touched its rim when the conversation ended.

'Σε πάμε σπίτι σου' both said, simultaneously. 'Μπορείς να κάτσεις στο παγκάκι μπροστά στο κτί- ριο.'

Mr Adamson translated that too. That the policemen would bring me home, and that I should wait on the bench outside the building. 'Say Efcharistó,' he said. 'It means thank you.'

'Efcharistó,' I said.

The young policeman pointed at my bone. 'Τί ναι αυτό?' He looked as if he'd a new suspicion, or even as if he was suddenly afraid of me.

Mr Adamson said it was a bone from a *Tyrannosaurus rex*, and I repeated his sentence. Both officers nodded and looked at the bone. They were suddenly sweating heavily.

We were silent. There was nothing more to say. It was quiet in the station. A single fly buzzed so loudly around the room, we all looked up at it. Once, when it stopped, both officers got up as if they'd been given the order to and — one with, the other without his cap — went outside. When they came back, they'd their bicycles with them. They closed the door, leant the bikes against the table and began cleaning the already spick-and-span mudguards. Then the frame, the pedals, the tail light.

Mr Adamson cleared his throat. 'I need to go!' he said quietly. 'Another thing. Bibi. I'll never be near her again. Look for her. Give her the suitcase. *She*'s allowed to open it. With regards from her Granda.' He looked at me with his bulging eyes. Was he fighting back tears? He bent down to my ear at any rate and whispered, 'Maybe they do hear me, those two.' He looked around at the two policemen who, unaffected however, continued to rub at their bikes.

'I'll never see you again. It's too risky. For you, and for me. Never again, until. Fare well.'

He turned and walked through the closed door. Gone, he was. I gasped for air. He was leaving me alone with these two monsters! These two oafs! They weren't bothering about me. The young one, as he polished his bell, stuck his tongue out, he was so keen, and the old one was panting heavily as he tested the tension of the spokes. I went outside and sat on the bench. The sun was rising. It took a while for my eyes to get used to the bright light again. Mr Adamson was walking, far away already, on the straight-as-a-poker path between the olive trees. In the background, the small hill shone. Mr Adamson was running, yes, he was veritably bombing off so that I could barely see more than his behind. As if he were in a panic, the reason for which I couldn't see. I gulped. He couldn't do that to me! He couldn't just leave me sitting there, all on my own. The scoundrel!

He was now at the first bend in the mule track that led steeply up to the acropolis of the old Mycenae. He was now going much more slowly, however. He was dragging himself up there laboriously, putting one foot in front of the other. He was as small as a thumb but I could clearly see he had his mouth open and that his tongue was hanging out far. I was boiling with rage. The traitor! He was aban-

doning me in my greatest need! I was still a child after all!
I couldn't speak any Greek! How was I supposed to find
my way home without him? — He was stumbling now, stag-
gering from stone to stone. The path was also steep, after
all. His knees caved in as if they were no longer part of
him. Clinging to spurs of rock, he was taking longer and
longer breaks. He was no longer making any progress.

Finally, I grasped what was happening. He was losing
all his strength, slumping within. Once and for all, and
until the end of all time, *because I no longer loved him*. Suddenly,
I felt horrified.

I couldn't stand by and watch him not make it home.
To the entrance, I mean. Who would fetch me when the
time came?! I immediately tried to recall, in downright
panic, all the moments, the hours, when I'd loved him with
all my heart. When we played hide and seek! When we
walked down to the tram, singing! When we ran away
from the ancient old men in Tellstrasse and, from the tram,
saw the raging old men brandishing their crutches. Whenever we sat on the bench beside each other.

Internally pumping heat into my heart, I refused to let
Mr Adamson out of my sight. Right enough, he seemed to
recover and to be taking firmer steps again. He'd soon be

walking upright. He'd now reached the Lion Gate. He ran along the final metres of the cyclopean wall and was soon back at our old place. Yes, I liked him and it didn't matter any more if I thought he was a scoundrel. He'd been saved. 'Blackguard!' I roared, without any inhibition now. 'What about me?'

Mr Adamson stood before the old walls and waved. I could see his raised arm. I raised an arm too. He turned and vanished into the stones. The castle of Mycenae was again as still and timeless beneath the insistent sun as it had been for thousands of years already.

I haven't seen Mr Adamson again since. Or rather — no. One single time, I did. Many years later. Many years ago now. Just briefly, very briefly, and he was so different, I sometimes think it wasn't him at all. That it was some darkly perturbed doppelgänger. I'm certain the next time will be the one when —. Now, as I tell his story, I'm looking out for him. Anxiously, and with a certain longing. If I disregard that one time, it's now eighty-six years since I last saw him.

Naturally, I haven't forgotten Mr Adamson. Not ever. Course not. In the first weeks after I got home, I didn't stop thinking about him. Could see him around the corner of every house and turned with fright—or, who knows, delight—if ever I heard an unusual sound behind me. With time, however, his image faded, and years came along when I barely thought of him. Many of these years passed. A life. It once promised to last almost for ever and blew past like a sharp gust of wind.

The return journey from Mycenae was the kind of adventure even a Navajo rarely survives. I still had the magic feather in my hair, thank God, and the bone protected me. At any rate, the younger of the two policemen suddenly pushed his brightly polished bicycle out through the door and sat on the saddle. The old one grabbed me and set me on the pannier rack. "Ετοιμοι!' he said, giving his young colleague a slap on the back, who cycled off so fiercely and with such a wobble that I screamed—was it fear? or excitement?—and put my arms around his stomach. To be exact, I held on tight to the bone that I'd put across his front. The old policeman ran, panting, with a redder and redder face, alongside us until his colleague steadied up and swiftly took off. I looked back and saw him in the middle of the path. He'd a hanky as large as a flag in his hand and was waving. I didn't dare to let go of the bone that was now against my pilot's stomach, then I did and waved too, briefly, quickly. And yet, for a second, I lost my balance such that I almost fell from my seat, forcing the bike to tilt dangerously. We swerved from one edge of the path to the other. The young policeman swore. But then he'd his vehicle under control again, and soon we were veritably flying along. On our right, and left, olive trees whizzed past. Sheep, stone dwellings, here and there a farmer or his wife watching, baffled, as this odd fare passed. The policeman was singing now, a melody reminiscent of the call to prayer of a mosque crier, bearing in mind I'd never heard a muezzin. Using his bicycle bell, he was, to create a faster and faster rhythm. Soon, I was singing along, but more like a Navajo, not a Turk or a Saracen. Chickens fled as we approached. The stones on the path sprayed in all directions. For a time, a dog followed us but, though its head was stretched right out and its tongue hanging out, it couldn't match the now-devilish speed of my chauffeur and was left way behind. Its barks sounded farther and farther away. The policeman, letting loose, called something over his shoulder that, even though it was Greek, I understood. 'Yes, hammer it!' I screamed in reply, excited. 'Go faster!' We were now hurtling along such that I hugged the stomach of my saviour even more firmly, pressed one cheek against his back, closed my eyes and, open-mouthed, breathed the hot air that the airstream was unable to cool, and it was burning my lungs.

We sped along and, as I recall it, it was as if the policeman, whizzing through the air like a whirlwind—a blue sea, far below us—had me home again in no time. The last few metres, at any rate, he completed on the road again—I'm sure I remember that?—riding with no hands, his arms out wide like Jesus or the winner of the Alps stage of the Tour de France. He stopped at the garden gate, let me get off, said, 'Φτάσαμε!', touched his cap in salute—yes, he'd his cop's cap on!—turned and cycled off. Like a kamikaze, he disappeared into the abyss of the road, up ahead towards the white lady's house.

My mama and papa came rushing out of the house. My papa was faster, first to hug me and he started sobbing. The tears ran over his three-day stubble and splashed onto me. A father who cries! My mama, when my papa let me go finally, hugged me so tight, I was in danger of suffocating. 'Help!' I gasped, also because the bone was stuck between us. My mama was so out of her mind, she didn't notice the hardness between herself and me.

'What happened?' they both screamed. 'Two days! Two nights!' My papa was upset, worried, in a way I'd never seen, and my mama was wringing her hands. 'Simply gone!'

Of course, I'd promised Mr Adamson—my sacred
Indian oath—not to betray him, especially if, as was the
case, I was wearing my chief's feather and observing the
laws of the Navajos that stipulated you'd be burnt at the
stake if you ever revealed a secret. What I'd experienced,
though, had really rattled me—both my heart and my
behind. The latter was hurting terribly, the pannier rack
on the policeman's bike having consisted of three or four
hard-as-hell metal bars and, clinging to the policeman's
back, I'd been bumped up and down all the way home. I
wasn't capable of lying to my mama, my papa, this dear
papa who was looking at me through wet eyes, and my
mama, whose warm breath I could feel in my hair. I had
to tell the truth! So I told them how I'd got to know Mr
Adamson in the garden of Mr Kremer's villa. A nice old
man with an upper lip that looked like the porch outside
our front door, a bald skull with three stiff hairs, and bulging
eyes. How we'd played tig and hide and seek. How quickly
he could bomb along, how nimbly. How I'd fallen into him
and he'd been as transparent as a light curtain. How he'd
told me he was dead. My pre-deceased. How I, inside him,
had managed the entrance to another world though this is
an impenetrable wall for us mortals. What the other world
was like: dark, and filled with air that was like mucus, yet

mucus you could breathe. I was now sitting on my mama's lap and recalling, sometimes crying, at times trembling, how overpowering music had hurled me through a netherworld, up and down that universe. How Mr Adamson had fluttered around me, yet also seemed to be a plaything in the hands of the terrible energies that robbed me of my senses. How I waded through blood—'No, Papa, Mama, no, I wasn't dead!'—walking towards a silent wall of souls condemned for ever. (Now I'd escaped from them, I could see them more clearly than back then, when at their mercy.) Of those billions and billions who, unlike Mr Adamson now still, weren't allowed back up again and would soon be in absolute shadow for ever. How they all looked similar—green or grey, with dead eyes and mouths curling down—and yet each was different from the others. Looked the same, that said, in terms of being lost. In as much as they'd all taken leave of their senses, were incredibly alone, permanently lonely and comfortless. How there wasn't a hint of love in them, and their rage, their anger, their wanting to kill had no heart in it. This snapping of teeth, this desire to kill by biting was like a nervous twitch, a reflex at most, a memory perhaps, and so the deadly bites were half-hearted and missed me, even when they got closer and closer, became more and more targeted, more and more general. At some point, they were all biting close to me and in the end — I told them all this, and, more and more, it seemed I could remember every detail — it was inevitable that one of the blind and unsure bites would connect. And tear me to shreds. How I was suddenly inspired to sing. ('You sang?' my papa stammered, as if coming to again, after an anaesthetic. I nodded. 'I thought if I sang, they might not do anything to me.') How, after a period of cold panic, I escaped from the dead and now took a path that was indeed flatter. How newly dead people drifted past like stones or sacks, led by their escorts, hopping alongside them. That, from high above, those who were dead, once and for all, looked like a greyish-green carpet that, swaying gently, vanished far ahead over the horizon. Beyond that, no doubt, were still more dead people. Without doubt, the dead filled the interior of the entire globe; and entrances on Easter Island or Australia, too, led for sure into this one realm of the dead. In Earth's interior, there was no magma, and certainly not the Christian Hell. That was where the dead were.

'Oh, son!' my mama said, breaking into tears.

I buried my neck even deeper between her breasts. She stroked my hair. The feather fell onto the floor next to me. 'The feather!' I screamed, sitting up straight. 'I need the feather!' My papa bent down and handed it to me. I put it back in my hair without, I think, saying thank you.

'Then we got to the surface of Earth,' I continued. 'The rest you know. The policeman brought me home.'

My papa, in a way I didn't associate with him, was now running around the table—we were sitting in the kitchen—and each time he passed the fridge, he hammered his fist against the metal door. Finally, he stopped and looked at me in despair. 'All well and good,' he said. *'But how did you get to Mycenae?'*

'Haven't I just told you!' I said. 'Look!' I pointed at my feet. 'The blood's still there.'

My papa stared at my shoes, blue Bata trainers with yellow rubber soles to which black dried blood stuck. 'That's tar,' he said. He sat down at the table and buried his head in his arms. His shoulders were twitching.

'What Papa means,' my mama said in her gentlest voice. 'We got a phone call, you see. We didn't understand where from but it sounded far away. They'd found you, they said. There has to be some explanation for it.'

I looked from one to the other. My blind papa and my mama, who now hugged me even tighter. My back could

feel her heart. They hadn't understood a single word! And
yet I'd explained it all to them so precisely!

We sat there for a while, silent. Then I slipped down
from her lap, took the bone, went out of the door, up the
stairs and into my room. I lay there, with the bone by my
side, on the bed, staring at the ceiling till I fell asleep. I
vaguely felt someone, my mama, putting a cover over me
and when I woke during the night, the bedside lamp was
on. Both Papa and Mama were sitting next to me, like the
time before when I'd had that terrible brain fever and
thought I was going to die because it was Friday.

The next day already, a Tuesday probably, my papa took
me to see a doctor, a—as I realize now—psychiatrist or
child psychologist who had his practice on Blumenrain,
opposite the restaurant Zur blauen Rose that, much later,
would belong to one of my classmates at secondary school.
The doctor, a Dr Ackermann or Ackeret, or maybe even
Acklin, asked me to stack up some building bricks—my
papa was waiting in the next room—and showed me ink
blots in which, right away, even the greatest idiot would be
able to see a butterfly or my papa being bitten by dogs. Dr
Ackermann nodded, pleased, when I told him my diagnosis.

He went on to ask me this and that—how things were with my mama, did I like her—and then I was back outside and walking hand-in-hand with my papa, down Blumenrain to Schifflände, where we sat on the terrace of Confiserie Spillmann and looked down onto the Rhine. Ships sailed by and every now and then a swimmer drifted past. We both had an ice cream, a scoop of strawberry and of lemon each, a combination to which, to this day, I've remained loyal. The options can include every exotic fruit you can imagine—mango, passion fruit, kiwi, jaboticaba—and I'll stick tenaciously to strawberry and lemon. Noëmi, who is a rebel, occasionally has peach or that modern Häagen-Dazs stuff. But Anni keeps the tradition going, almost as consistently as I do. Bembo and Bimbo too: strawberry and lemon like their great-granda.

Once home, I let go of my papa's hand. We'd not spoken of my adventure on the way back, nor did we later. In the many years that followed—Papa and Mama got old—not one of us mentioned my odyssey. Only—but when did that ever happen—when the name Mycenae came up, or Schliemann, did our lives seem to pause for the hint of a moment. We'd look at one another in that special way, or not at all, which confirmed for each that the other was also thinking of that black moment in life. But then our normal racket would resume.

I bolted — my papa having gone into the house — over to Mick, who was crouched beside the fish pond in his garden and in the process of fishing out the dead tadpoles. He bred frogs. Never, however, did a single tadpole of his grow to be a frog. Somehow, they all died as children and swam on their backs or were pecked out of the water by birds. To Mick, who could read me like a book otherwise — as I could him — I said not a word. Even though he would never have betrayed me. I hadn't told anyone about his adventure with the man in the park either, only my mama, and even my papa knew about my visit to the netherworld. With time, I myself forgot about it, thought I'd merely dreamt it. It was just that my shoes were still at the back of the cupboard, beneath old junk, with the same blood on the soles that got black and blacker until it did indeed look like old tar.

Until now, Anni, I've simply been talking to myself, to no one in particular, to everyone, but I'm becoming increasingly sure I'm telling *you* all this. The story of Mr Adamson, who also had a granddaughter. I now know — now that I'm a granda myself, a great-granda even — how much his heart must have been burning when, with my help, he tried to find out what had become of his Bibi. Whether she was well, and how. And yet she'd only have been twelve at the time. A girl still. All the more exciting it would be for Mr Adamson today to learn what life and its relentlessness had later made of her. But that's just it: there will always be some people in your long line of successors whose future you'll never know. Because they're part of a generation after you. That's painful, but sometimes also better that way.

Don't worry, Anni, I don't intend to tell you my life story. Let's sum it up this way: it was one birthday after another. First, I blew the candles out; then Susanne and I did the blowing; then Susanne and Noëmi—and me a few too; then Noëmi and you, Anni; and finally you and Bembo and Bimbo. I looked at the green leaves of the lime tree outside the house and when next I looked, the leaves, now red, were falling to the ground. At a similar speed, my hair fell out. First, black hair. Then, grey hair. Soon, white hair.

I hope, incidentally—otherwise, it's all been a waste!— you find the recorder here on the bench. It's yours, after all. And I hope you also notice I've spoken into it, have filled it up. You *must* realize, surely, I didn't want your recording device for no reason at all. Great piece of kit, incidentally. Really. In my younger years I had a UHER,

which was regarded back then as a miracle of miniaturiza-
tion, the size of a brick and twice as heavy. And now your
technological masterpiece. The size of two cubes of sugar
and able to hold ten thousand hours of material.

So, Anni. I need to tell you still about my two—what
to call them?—quirks. Otherwise, you won't understand
how inexorably my life has remained linked, to this day,
with the shadowy existence of Mr Adamson. They kept
me on board, these follies. Kept the link with Mr Adamson
going. These two obsessions—which controlled me, as you
will see, up to a clearly identifiable date—were: the language
of the Navajos. Plus, I used to dig. They were Mr Adamson's
legacy, so to speak, and also a kind of obedience with which
I followed the ancient pointer of my gods who had put a
bone my way, the magic and remarkableness of which burnt
my palms back then, and still do. As if magma had spat it
out. Look, here, this is the bone, it's glowing hot. You saw
it in the car. 'What's that, Granda?' you asked. I answered,
'The bone of a mammoth. Or of a *Tyrannosaurus rex.*' You
laughed and said, 'It's that of a cow.' You were probably
right.

So, the language of the Navajos waylaid me, like an illness. A beautiful addiction. A sweet mania. Firstly, for sure,
because it beat every language I'd ever encountered in

terms of complexity. Secondly, of course, because for as long as I could remember, I'd been a Navajo myself, a chief even, and I cherished the chief's feather even as an adult. It lay for all those years in the second-top drawer of my desk, among old photographs and drawings Noëmi did as a child, a scrubby relic that I'd never have thrown out. One doesn't dispose of sacred feathers! Today, I'm wearing it in the last three hairs remaining on my head. On an impulse, I fetched it from the drawer before I left and, for the whole trip here, could see it in the mirror of the Citroën. I can feel it now as I touch it with two fingers: the feather worn by every chief at his enthronement (Mick enthroned me and I, him) and that accompanies him to the Eternal Hunting Grounds.

Anyone setting out—I was in my mid-twenties when I did—to learn the language of the Navajos with a view to, one day, commanding it fully, has lost that battle before he even starts. Correct Diné-Bizaad doesn't exist and has perhaps never existed because, like the language of chameleons, it consists of deviations and variations that, as soon as they are formed, are immediately varied again, in new deviations. An ancient language, and it has always been that way. From the year Dot. If you learn one exception, you've been overlooking another, then you confuse the third with the fourth that, in any case, people aren't saying any more by the time you stumble upon it. It's the same for the Navajos themselves though. Like anywhere else in the world, the children, while babbling away to themselves, master the most absurdly complex constructions with ease. They don't even notice they're using the continuous imperfect, which drove the likes of me to despair. Diné-Bizaad — the Navajos call themselves *Diné*, human beings — is indeed so incomprehensible that, in the Second World War, the US army employed twenty-seven Navajos as sergeants in its department of radio communications. They were more efficient than any code system, speaking to one another quite normally. The Japanese, who decoded every other communication mode, didn't understand — right up to the last day of hostilities — a word of the inscrutable sounds they were picking up and that — as they guessed — were directing the troops in the Pacific. Without the Navajos, Guam, Iwo Jima, Okinawa, Peleliu, Saipan, Bougainville and Tarawa would never have been taken. And the Navajo radio operators, once the war had been won, received high military honours that, along with their traditional magic objects (wolf paws, bear teeth, prairie dog skulls) they wore on special occasions. — That's a long time ago already,

Anni. Have *you* heard of Pearl Harbour or Hiroshima? More likely not, I suppose.

I'd soon become addicted to my hunt for the language of the Navajos even if, over a period of years and decades, I met no one who shared the same passion or was even a Navajo Indian. There were no Indians in Basel. I didn't let myself be put off, however, and spoke to my reflection. I'd no idea whether the answers it gave were comprehensible to anyone but me. I reckoned, at any rate, that my mirrored self was pretty good at Diné-Bizaad and I replied with highly risky attempts at sentences. I used, above all, Robert Young and William Morgan's *The Navajo Language* (1943); later, of course, the expanded reprint (Desert Press 1967); and Alan Wilson's *Breakthrough Navajo* (University of Mexico, 1969). I ignored—in order not to overstretch myself as I took my first steps—the fact that every clan pronounces things differently; and that, roughly speaking, there are eight hundred and twenty clans. (Of course, every Navajo knew at the drop of a hat which clan his interlocutor belonged to.) To begin with, I didn't bother either with the fact that—as Irvy W. Goossen puts it—'changes within the verb lead to a huge vocabulary.' That was probably true: to a really huge one, even. Nor did I let myself be affected by Alan Wilson, who warned that every non-native speaker who tried to speak to the Navajos in their tongue triggered, without fail, almost uncontrollable laughter in everyone present. They'd double up with laughter, the Navajos, and whatever you said next would unleash another gale of laughter. 'The Navajos laugh a lot': a view expressed in all the textbooks but, as I now know, fallacious. The Navajos didn't have a lot to laugh about; so little, in fact, that even attempts by the likes of us to intone their nasals correctly were a source of great enjoyment. (To produce them, a little air must flow through the nose. A little! Not a lot. And not hardly any, either.) It was amusing, for sure, if someone like me was trying to say *béésh bee hane'i* ('the metal with which you tell stories', so a phone) and instead said 'an unkempt hairbrush' because his intonation was slightly higher or rising on the final *i*. —I had difficulty with glottal pauses too, especially as I never got to the bottom of what exactly a glottal pause was. It was something, at any rate, that no one who wasn't an Indian managed to produce (not even Goossen and Wilson) and it was the most common of all the consonants. It was even the case that all the words that appeared to begin with a vowel in fact started with a glottal pause. So I tried—in front of the mirror, with me myself as my partner—to produce the glottal consonants /*ch*', *k*', *t*', *tl*'/ by, as the textbook recommended, preparing my mouth for the consonant and then releasing it with a closed glottis. I also ensured that I produced these high sounds by using air from my mouth, rather than my lungs. And when I said /gh/, I imagined—as *Navajo Made Easier* recommended—I'd a hair in the roof of my mouth that I wanted to get rid of. For hours I formed the /l/, expelling the air between the sides of my tongue and my palate. Again and again, always afresh, and I hadn't the faintest idea whether I was doing it right or wrong.

You perhaps remember my second quirk, Anni. That I used to dig. You were with me more than once when I was in the garden with my dirty trousers and my tools. Yes, I dug. For many years, I couldn't see a spade without sticking it into the soil. An uncontrollable urge. Digging did my head good in that—this is what I call happiness!—it had absolutely nothing to do, to think about, while the rest of my body sweated and boiled. I was happy to settle for ploughing up the garden and planting potatoes. (At times, you, a little girl, collected those beetles in a toy bucket that Mick's father called *Leptinotarsa decemlineata*.) Each time my heart whirred—so daily, really—I grabbed my spade and off into the garden. I was instantly happy. I became the fool that fortune favoured—for I'd the biggest potatoes far and wide. Susanne was pleased too, became a champion at potato dishes. Gratin dauphinois, pommes allumettes, fried potatoes done in lard. You enjoyed them too. Do you remember?

I thought, of course, about Mr Adamson any time I used my spade. But I'd no Mr Stamatakis, and no Schliemann either, to dig for, and in Basel and the surrounding area, very lucky diggers found, at best, fossilized toilet facilities from the Early Middle Ages or, at most, a few Celtic sherds. I admit that, right at the beginning of my enthusiastic garden drudgery, split-second images would occasionally flash before my eyes of marble columns bathed in light, of groves, of radiant white temples. Very clearly, I was dreaming of Greece, which I hadn't seen since my adventure with Mr Adamson. A royal tomb was, indeed, a different matter than a potato. I began to think that, even if Mycenae had been reconnoitred meanwhile, many a beautiful thing still had to be hidden in other places. Olympia, I'd heard, was still a meadow with a few marble ruins peeking, at an angle, out of the ground. I did then travel, with Susanne and my army-patent spade attached to my belt to Athens, to Epidaurus, to Naxos and Paros, to Mycenae too. I immediately found the entrance of the dead and felt around the old walls. On one occasion, I also felt that shivering when — without a doubt — a dead person walked through me. After that, I wanted to go straight home. We began our return journey a few days

earlier than planned. I was a digger, yes, but not an archae-
ologist. Feeling in no way pained, I returned to my potatoes.

Then though, from one minute to the next, I stopped digging.
You'd just turned nine at the time. I put my spade down,
and that was it. My mission — permit the pathos — had been
fulfilled. I suddenly knew why I'd learnt to dig every kind
of ground like the clappers, even the stoniest; and why I'd
tried so hard to learn the language of the Navajos properly.
Yes, even with the Navajos, it was now all over. The purpose
of my endeavours, which had seemed preposterous to everyone around me and, at times, even to me myself — how
Noëmi had made fun of her a-little-crazy Papa! — had
become clear.

I can put it another way, Anni. For I had one last brief
and tempestuous affair, for the duration of which the digger
and the Navajo in me were on fire. The lover in me too,
possibly. A flood of emotions like I'd not expected to feel
again. On 4 September 2011 (an unforgettable date for all
of us; for me, though, not just because the Israel–Palestine
reconciliation was sealed) I met a woman, you see. — Yes,
Anni. I know what you're thinking. Check him out, the
randy so-and-so. Like the old Goethe, he wants his Ulrike.

112

But I was only Goethe's age, seventy-three. And my Ulrike, who was called Daphne, wasn't sixteen but about eighty. And if, after three wild nights and two hot days I was on the boil like the old Goethe, then not for those reasons.

At any rate, I was in the restaurant Zum braunen Mutz, having a beer after work. (I'd come straight from the field.) A woman swung the door open as if she wanted to reduce it to splinters and made a beeline for my table. For an ancient old woman, she was pretty energetic. Casting a shadow over the entire table, she sat down opposite me. She was breathing hard. She looked like a hobgoblin, like a gnome that turned out as a giant. Her face was held together by countless wrinkles—like they were mooring ropes. Behind thick spectacle lenses, two Basedow eyes that, hugely magnified, were gawping at me. Hair, she didn't have any more, so to speak. The three white strands growing on her pink skull were tied together in a bun, made from a handful of hair. Add to that a khaki blouse, a brown woollen skirt, red socks emerging from hefty mountain boots. She ordered a Féchy. Half a litre. I drank my beer and by the time I ordered another, she'd knocked back her wine and was ordering a second half litre. I took no notice of her—you get a lot of women boozing in the Mutz—and used the anonymous din in the place to memorize the verb for 'to bark' in the Navajo tongue. *Nahal'in*, he barks. *Naháháliih*, he barks repeatedly or untiringly. *Nahóóliich*, he has barked. *Nahohoofiil*, he will bark.

'Navajo?' the woman said. Her eyes were already glassing over somewhat.

Obviously, forgetting myself, I'd muttered to myself or moved my lips, at least. I got such a fright, I almost fell off my seat.

'Diné-Bizaad,' I said. 'Do you speak the language of the Navajos?'

'Fluently,' she said.

That wasn't true, it turned out. She didn't understand, in any case, a word of what I said to her. And I was speaking especially clearly, over-articulating the glottal pauses. She shook her head. I, though, could understand what I was saying perfectly well and went so far—now that I'd a listener for the first time—as to produce the most complex of sentence constructions. I began to feel a real high. The woman looked at me with eyes, if it was possible, that were getting bigger still. Finally, she applauded, with her large paws. 'You're my man, young man! Sent from Heaven!' she said in the middle of a sentence that was promising to turn out particularly splendidly. 'I have reason to celebrate today! Cheers!'

'Cheers!' I said, in German, lifting my glass.

She rummaged around in her skirt and pulled out a business card. 'Daphne Miller, Dr h. c. mult'. I think I looked at her, pretty baffled.

'That's me,' she said. 'Since yesterday. Dr h. c. mult, I mean. Amazing, isn't it? The *mult* is what gives it its ring. Until now, I was just an ordinary h. c. And one in every two people you meet is that.' She smiled, as if considering the possibility I could be such a person. 'I had the cards printed. I've just come from the print shop. Not even twenty francs for a thousand cards. You're the first to get one. You can keep it.'

'Thanks,' I said, putting the card away.

If I understood correctly what Mrs Miller now spouted forth—sounding really local, with no hint of an English accent—the Catholic Academy in Passau had informed her by letter that it wished to confer an honorary doctorate on her. (She already had one, from the University of Edinburgh. Top address.) And so she'd travelled to Passau—from Phoenix, Arizona, a long way—and at a very dignified ceremony in a room full of crucifixes, the honorary doctor's hat was placed on her head. The award was for her life's work, all undertaken outside academia. She was something like an ethnologist, even if she didn't give a toss how the guild defined the term. She simply did everything that seemed important for her work and didn't spurn the spade-work involved, even. 'I've excavated any number of graves,' she said, 'and transferred the relics of the assassins.' Stands to reason, I began to listen carefully. She was working—when I realized *that*, my excitement was boundless—in the ancestral homeland of the Navajos. In the Four Corners region, where the four federal states of New Mexico, Arizona, Colorado and Utah meet. (She'd ended up there because she—a child of my home town; indeed, almost a child still—had married a Mr Miller, who dragged her off to his homeland and soon upped and left with another woman.) Her base was in Window Rock, Arizona, a sort of capital for the Navajos, where she'd been staying in the same motel for decades. (The letter from Passau had also reached her there. She then drove her Toyota pickup the three hundred miles to the airport of Phoenix, Arizona.)

The Indians fascinated her so much that, even when Mr Miller vanished from her life, she remained in their ancestral homeland. She wasn't interested in Indian folklore, though, in old customs or the relations between clans but was looking for memories, traces, of the final freedom struggles. When it was that the pride of the Indians—though they'd now long been petrol-pump attendants, barkeepers or bus drivers—was deeply offended, and what they then did. When—for brief, high moments—did they confuse their existence with the glorious past, those days when, all in war paint, they'd ridden horses as fast as the wind. She didn't bother with the heroic battles of yore. Summit Springs and Sand Creek. No, her interest was in the dreary little revolts of still somehow recent years, that had been about freedom and resembled pub brawls that had left this one or that one dead on the battlefield. Apart from her, no one had addressed these almost invisible explosions of rage and despair. She'd even been present at one, soon after her arrival in Window Rock, during her honeymoon with Mr Miller, so to speak. A smashed-up bar, a dead tourist from Vermont, whose scalp his murderer, a nineteen-year-old Navajo, had tried to remove but without knowing the technique of his forefathers, with the result that, when the police turned up with their sirens wailing, the young hero was in tears and on his knees beside his blood-bathed victim, surrounded by the helpless customers of the trashed bar, among them Mrs Miller. *She* knew how to scalp someone properly, even back then, but hadn't had an opportunity to tell the young man. The sheriff was faster. The murderer was taken away and sentenced to death and the whole affair was soon forgotten.

Mrs Miller's interest, though, had been ignited. She'd been working ever since on an exhaustive documentation of such incidents and, working back from the then present, had already reached the period before the Second World War. 'I'm now working on a case from 1938,' she said. 'A different calibre. A dozen dead, and no one's prepared to say a word. — Shall I tell you something?' She was now flaring like a torch. 'There's cost involved! No Indian will speak to you for free! The motel wants four hundred bucks a month!' She snorted. 'And they give me an honorary doctorate, these papists, with zero dosh! The honour alone. I'm living off the pension of one thousand, one hundred and thirty francs I'm entitled to per month. — *See what I mean*?' she added, in English.

'So am I!' I said, fired up in the same way she was. 'Three thousand, one hundred and five francs for both of us — Susanne and me. The apartment alone costs four thousand. We live off whatever's left! — Look. I used to dig too.'

I raised my bone to show her. I had it with me, as I always did back then. She looked at it with her eyes screwed tight.

'*Tyrannosaurus rex*?' she asked.

'Cow!' I should've —shouldn't I, Anni?—answered. 'Or a mammoth,' I said instead.

It turned out, she was only warming up, here in the Mutz. She was getting her strength up for a celebration to be held in her honour. Today. Right now, actually. The doyenne of what all those who weren't part of it called the Single Malt Circle—for the best brains in it loved drinking premium whisky—had tracked her down in Passau, on her mobile, just as—with her newly acquired doctor's hat on her head—she was explaining to the bishop the rituals involved when the Apaches burn someone at the stake. (The bishop was beaming blissfully.) The doyenne of the circle implored her with a syrupy voice to drop by. 'Tomorrow! Won't you? Informal attire, of course!' She wouldn't regret it, everyone was looking forward hugely to her coming.

Mrs Miller had actually wanted to fly straight back to Phoenix—her current case was close to being solved—but it was the first time the circle had shown any interest in her; that the elite of the town where she'd grown up had bothered with her work. For the Single Malt Circle was such a hermetically sealed society that no one, not even its members, knew *exactly* who the members were. (Its members never spoke about the Single Malt Circle. They said *we*. '*We*'ll be lowering the death duties next year. *We*'re blocking Augustinerstrasse to private cars. *We*'re increasing the number in the symphony orchestra to 112.') And indeed, invited to the celebration were all those who, until now, hadn't even ignored Mrs Miller; or who, in the better-case scenario, had scoffed at her without inhibition. Emeritus professors, lawyers, a member of the governing council (an ultra-conservative woman) and the local monied aristocracy (chemical industry, banking). 'Not one of them has ever said hello, even!' she champed with rage. 'And yet I'm here every year for carnival! Every year!' She was speaking so loudly now, customers at the neighbouring tables were staring. 'They're swimming in money, that lot! I *have* to go!'

The Single Malt Circle met on the first Wednesday of every month and always at the doyenne's house. Today was the first Wednesday of the month. Mrs Miller had no idea how her hostess had got wind of the honour so soon and how, above all, she'd got her mobile number that— with the exception of a few Navajo chiefs—no one actually had. Her hostess had her ear to all the bush drums. She was ninety, approximately, and lived on the interest on the interest of a fortune her father had left her when she was still almost a child. She could get by on this as her lifestyle wasn't especially extravagant. A villa with six or seven rooms, a garden full of rhododendrons and that was about it. No husband for decades now. No dog. For supper, she always had three radishes. And no salt.

'I promised, faithfully, I'd be there by half past seven,' Mrs Miller said, looking, concerned, at the clock above the door of the beer hall, which was showing a quarter to nine. She sighed, waved to the waiter, paid, heaved herself up and reached for her stick. 'Was a pleasure,' she said.

'I'll drive you there!' I said, also jumping up. 'I'm here with the car.'

It—the Citroën ZX, even back then—was parked right outside the bar. Mrs Miller opened the door as if this had always been the plan and sat beside me, on the passenger seat, like an Inca. With absolute certainty, she directed me through the town, to the right, left, straight ahead, get into this lane here—as if I were a stranger. And yet, with every metre we drove, *I* knew my way around better. We drove past the station, you see, over the bridge crossing the railway lines, past Margarethenpark, and then—on the steep street full of bends—up to the plateau, high above the town, where I lived as a child. You know, of course, where I live now, Anni. At the other end of town. And I'd, indeed, not been up there for an eternity. Naturally, everything was now smaller, the streets were shorter and narrower, and there were no meadows any more. Everywhere where once there had been cornfields, there were now villas with double garages. Stubs of streets with turning bays at the end. Everything was very different. Yet I was driving more and more surely, and feeling more and more certain, quite unlike Mrs Miller whose commands were getting more and more contradictory. It turned out that not only had she never been up here but she'd also forgotten the address of her hostess. She knew her name, true—it didn't mean anything to me—but, otherwise, only that her house was white, had no windows, so to speak, and was at the top end of the street that led up to the town's highest point. That was why the water tower was also nearby, the water needs a bit of momentum if there's to be decent pressure as it flows from the taps.

My heart was suddenly pounding. Yes, yes, I knew where I had to go. While Mrs Miller was looking around as nervously as a jackrabbit lost in the forest and saying, 'Right. No, left. There, up there! No, here!' I, paying no attention to her, homed in on my childhood street. Here too, the headlights of the ZX lit up villas I'd never seen before. But the old houses from back then were still there too: Richi Wanner's house, the Gross family's house and Mr Henkel's, in whose garden, at one time, a really dangerous Alsatian had always hounded along the fence, such that I'd do detours of miles and miles to avoid it. I went back down into second gear and drove up the so incredibly familiar street with the now-listless Mrs Miller at my side. I stopped outside the home of the white lady. 'We're there,' I said.

'On whose say-so!' Mrs Miller said, waking from her dreams. 'It wasn't so difficult after all!'

I got out. An iron gate. Behind it, as you could only guess, the silhouette of the house. Behind that, the black walls of Mr Kremer's villa loomed into the sky. No light there, course not. My former home was completely dark too, in the house where Mick had lived or perhaps still lived there wasn't a glimmer. A clear starry sky in which creatures were flying, bats perhaps, or owls.

The iron gate swung open without us ringing. Probably some sensor or other had noticed our arrival, or the sixth sense of the white lady had perceived us. The door of the house—open at the end of a path of granite slabs, lit by bright floodlights. The silhouette of a woman in the doorway. Mrs Miller raced ahead and I ran after her. I probably strayed from the most direct route a little for an alarm went off, that same siren I'd often heard as a child, daily actually, when the postman came or the Globus home delivery service brought a week's supply of radishes.

The white lady herself stood in person in the doorway. (You know, Anni, I'd hoped to tell this story without her. *No chance*, as they say in English.) She came towards us with wide open arms, all *Ah*!s and *Oh*!s and 'Don't worry about that noise, it's only the alarm, come in, carry on, carry on. Wonderful that you're dressed so informally, don't give it a thought, the other guests are also wearing whatever they're most comfortable in. I'll be right with you, Jean!' — this, to a young man standing behind her in a waiter's uniform and with a bottle of champagne in his hand — 'Jean, call the police. False alarm. It was the young man here, the companion. There's no danger! Everything's under control! You' — to Mrs Miller — 'are Mrs Miller! Welcome!' To me, 'And you're no doubt the husband!' And to Mrs Miller again, 'I didn't know, I'd no idea, of course, that you're married. How nice! How wonderful! Come closer.'

'He's my colleague,' Mrs Miller said. 'I don't know what I'd do without him.' She gave me a smile, a grin, actually.

In a large, brightly lit room, the windows of which were tiny portholes, twenty or even thirty ladies and gentlemen were standing around, all with glasses in their hands, and pausing their conversations to stare at Mrs Miller. The

ladies were wearing gowns with low necklines, the gentlemen were in black. One, a giant with horn-rimmed specta-
cles, put down his glass and applauded. They all followed
his lead, clapping so elegantly, I could barely hear a sound.
Many of the ladies were wearing gloves, silky soft gossamer
that made their applause completely inaudible. They were
all beaming, as if they were experiencing, right at this
moment, the most beautiful moment of their lives. Mrs
Miller stood with a bright red face and, allowing herself to
get carried away, even performed something like a curtsy.
'*Thank you*,' she said, in English. '*Thanks a lot.*'

She was immediately hogged by a few of the gentlemen
and I'd time to look around. Pictures of ancestors on the
wall, rugs. There were chairs — Louis XV perhaps — but
the guests were standing in groups or wandering around.
So much yackety-yack, you'd have thought you were in an
aviary or at the zoo. A beautiful woman, breaking into a
laugh. The stag-like bell of a red-in-the-face *bon vivant*. Jean
moved lizard-like among the guests who didn't ever look
at him, yet held their glasses in exactly the right angle. No
one was drinking whisky. That would come later, maybe.
At the rear was a wall of black windowpanes, behind which
was a further room, for sure. No light there.

I must've been looking a little lost for the white lady took mercy on me and came over. She was exactly as she'd been seventy years ago, except I'd never seen her so very close-up. Back then, she'd been a white shadow, a ghost that occasionally, rarely, had danced around between the tripwires in the garden when I'd peeked out of my dormer window. She was still as thin as a lath. A white lath. She smiled at me.

'And you? You give Mrs Miller a hand?'

'I do,' I said. 'We're inseparable.'

Something stopped me from telling her I used to live in the house opposite. Maybe because whenever, on my way home, I went into the garden of Mr Kremer's villa, I forced my way along so close to her garden wall, I felt it to be an encroachment. Something illicit and intimate. I pretended not to have seen her before. And she didn't recognize me.

'The alarm,' I said. 'Forgive me. Entirely my mistake.'

She explained that the area was crawling with burglars and murderers. No one could take a step around the outside of the house, not her either, without the police turning up five minutes later. She felt safe this way though she still couldn't sleep at night. For the alarm system didn't help against what really frightened her, what had been lurking in this house since the year Dot. 'The place is crawling with dead people,' she whispered, grabbing my hand. 'I can't see them. I can feel them. Everyone thinks I'm a hysterical old cow. No one believes me, and certainly not the police. You don't believe me either.'

'No, I do,' I said.

At that moment, behind the glass of the wall opposite, I saw the face of Mr Adamson. He was hanging, white, in the black glass, like the moon in the sky. Mr Adamson was staring at Mrs Miller—standing directly before him. His mouth was open and the three hairs on his skull pointing sharply upwards. His eyes were big and round. I rushed to the door in the glass wall so quickly, he only spotted me when we were nose to nose, with the glass between us. There was sheer horror on his face. He disappeared into the blackness in the room but I was through the door so fast that he didn't quite manage to escape. 'Mr Adamson!' I called to his back. 'Wait! Just wait!' He hid his face in his hands and ran as if chased by the Furies. 'I don't know you! I don't know him!' he gasped, vanishing into the wall.

I was standing, helpless, before the flame-patterned wallpaper of this gloomy room when his head came out of the wall again. So close to me that, in my shock, I took a step back.

'The woman over there,' he whispered, blinking across at the lit panes of glass, behind which the silhouettes of the white lady's guests could be seen. 'The one with the odd clothes. Who is she?'

'Mrs Miller,' I said, just as quietly. 'From Window Rock, Arizona.'

He looked at me doubtfully, despairingly. 'She reminds me of someone. But I don't know who.' He disappeared into the wall again. For good, this time.

I was standing in the empty salon that, as I now knew, was anything but empty. It was Louis-something-or-other too, the wallpaper at least, and also a solitary little table at the wall, the gold of which was flaking off. Here, the dead had their salon, close enough to the entrance for them to be able to enjoy being together with all the strength available to them and far enough away to be able to recover a little from the netherworld. That said, they had to stand, unless they made do with the parquet floor. The white lady could easily have put in a few chairs for them.

It was chilly here, cold almost, though outside it was the warmest September in human memory. The party of the dead was just as well attended as that of the white lady. A gloomy light, none actually, just a pale glow was coming through the windows. I staggered, two or three steps in the direction of the door, and fainted.

When I came to again, the white lady's face was hovering above me. Wrinkles, red lips, blue hair, brown teeth. She was observing me in an interested fashion. 'You're not the first,' she said when I raised my head. 'It happens to them all here. And they all report afterwards that they' had a near-death experience. Did you have a near-death experience?'

'No,' I said. I nodded to the invisible guests. 'It won't happen again. Enjoy the rest of your evening.'

The white lady looked at me, puzzled. 'You need a whisky,' she said. She led me over into the salon, holding me by the elbow as if I might drop to the floor again at any moment. Jean gave me a whisky that I drank in a oner. Single malt — no doubt about it. A sixteen-year-old, at least.

Mrs Miller now came running up to me. She'd not been aware of my misfortune. 'Let's scram!' she whispered. 'Before they regret it. They want to fund a whole year of my research and even your ticket.'

'What kind of ticket?' I said.

'*Business class*, man! — I told them I need you for my current case. There are a few things to be excavated. You'll get fifty dollars per day. Okay?'

I nodded. I don't know why. I nodded eagerly.

'Check-in is tomorrow morning at seven-thirty. Terminal B. American Airlines. Be on time.'

I said goodbye to the white lady who was blooming like life itself and wanted to shake the hands of all the ladies and gentlemen. They had now all moved on to the whisky—the ladies, too—and didn't notice me at all. Mrs Miller must have gone on ahead, the front door was open. That said, she wasn't at the car. 'Mrs Miller?' I called into the night but only a night bird in Mr Kremer's garden responded. I went back to the house and, of course, set off one of the alarms again that Jean, the waiter, again turned off. I didn't find Mrs Miller there either. She'd vanished into the night, said the white lady who had a triple single malt in her hand and was glowing like a red rose. I thanked her again, got into the ZX and drove home.

I left a note for Susanne on the kitchen table. 'Will call you.' I'd always been setting off for somewhere before, when I was still immortal or thought I was, even more often than in the years in question here. Nonetheless, that I was doing it again now wasn't *so* out of the ordinary. I had my mobile, after all. You know, Anni, getting up early isn't my strong point. This time though, oddly, it was easy. I was downright cheerful when at an unearthly hour I swung out of bed (Susanne was still sleeping; had already been sleeping when I'd got home; I couldn't bring myself to wake her) and set off with a small travel bag. The bone, I took with me, of course, and the Navajo feather too. And at the last moment, I attached my army-patent spade to my belt.

Mrs Miller was standing at the departure gate, dressed as she had been the day before. Apart from now having a rucksack, a field-grey monster, the kind of thing the first people to climb the Bietschhorn or the Dufour Peak had carried. She was beaming, she was downright radiant as she'd persuaded the lady at check-in to upgrade our tickets to First Class. No idea how she managed *that*; she'd a real talent for scrounging.

The flight, accordingly, was pleasant. We camped on cushions, surrounded by attentive flight attendants — champagne and club sandwiches: all you could drink and eat — and landed, bright-eyed and bushy-tailed, in Phoenix, Arizona. A thundering heat as we disembarked and walked across the apron, a cool air in the airport. The black Customs officer was as friendly as Uncle Tom. Welcomed me and found my papers to be flawless. And yet I'd only packed my passport! Probably, one of the Single Malt gents had called the president in Washington — and he'd used his red telephone to issue the instruction not to cause me and Mrs Miller any difficulty.

The Toyota was still there too, and soon we were on the Interstate 17 and rattling northwards. An at first white, then more and more yellow and, finally, red sun accompanied us to our left, over the horizon towards which it was slowly sinking. Behind her own wheel too, Mrs Miller looked like an Inca, like a very competent Inca for she drove with the authority of a Wild West truck driver. A landscape, the likes of which I'd never seen before, and yet it was deeply familiar to me. Treeless mountain ranges, washed-out canyons full of red scree. Desert-like plains. Withered shrubs, cacti. Here and there, a rattlesnake withdrawing lazily under a rock. Every two hours, a rusty petrol station.

When we left the Interstate and were driving on a smaller road full of potholes — beyond Lupton — Mrs Miller took two of the First Class sandwiches out of a bag and gave me one. That was our evening meal. A beer with it would have done me good. But Mrs Miller hadn't nicked any.

Finally, we were driving on a gravel path, a creek bed just about, that nonetheless was the main road leading into

Window Rock. The sun was going down just as we pulled up outside a broad, two-storey building. A balcony balustrade ran the full length of the upper floor. The whole house was ablaze in the red of the glowing sun and, as we climbed the steps to the entrance, the shadows of the night climbed the walls so quickly that the house was already in darkness. The sky burnt above its black silhouette. A neon sign began to flash. AVAJ MOTE. Mrs Miller's motel. The *N*, the *O* and the *L* were broken. Mrs Miller's room was on the first floor and I was given one at the other end of the hall. As I put the key in the lock, Mrs Miller, who — that far away — was fiddling about with her door, called, 'See you tomorrow. We're going to see Captain Briggs.' She pushed the door open and vanished.

My room: wood, dark, dusty air. A bed that almost filled the room. On the walls, Indian-looking objects as decoration. Moccasins, a bow and arrow, that kind of thing. I put my bag beneath the washbasin, opened the door to the balcony and stepped outside.

Beneath me, in the last of the dusk already, lay a square framed by the silhouettes of blockhouses. A few lights here and there, the brightly lit entrance to a bar — Jimmy's or Jonny's, I couldn't read it properly from up there — and directly beneath me was the Toyota and the wreck of a car, the four doors of which were wide open, as if the occupants hadn't taken the trouble to close them one last time. No one to be seen anywhere, even the bar was quiet. Only at the other end of the square, their backs against the wall of a chunky wooden house—filled the whole rear of the square, it did—sat four or five figures. Next to each other, motionless, barely discernible in the light of the pathetic garland of bulbs above their heads. They were Indians, for sure: they'd feathers on their heads. They looked like a squad of invalids, a silent reproach to fate, though they were just sitting there, saying nothing. The paint smeared on their faces, the red across their arms and legs too—was that warpaint?—There was also, as I could see now, a white man. He didn't look any better. An old-style trapper who'd also been given a raw deal.

I took my mobile out and called Susanne. It took a while for her to answer and her voice sounded sleepy.

'I'm in Window Rock,' I said.

'Where? Is that a bar?'

'It's the capital city of the Navajos.'

'At two in the morning?' she yawned. 'Take it you'll be back for breakfast?'

'More likely not,' I said.

The bar—Jimmy's or Jonny's—reminded me I was dying of thirst. Thankfully, I'd some dollars on me as Mrs Miller had paid me for my first day's work *in cash* and in the local currency. So I put my chief's feather in my hair and went downstairs and diagonally across the square to the bar. Jamie's, not Jimmy's. The group of scarecrows outside the dark blockhouse—the city hall, presumably, and so the seat of the authorities—had disappeared, apart from one, an Indian who, in full warpaint, was standing in the middle of the square. He was small, much smaller than me, had a few singed feathers on his head, a face covered in blood and a smashed arm. His clothes were hanging on him, in tatters. What on earth had happened to him?

He was standing on a flat hill of earth, barely a few palms high, a kind of trampled-flat tumulus that car tracks criss-crossed, and he looked at me, not that I'd stopped in front of him, with that Indian's expression I knew only too well and had never yet encountered. Inscrutable. I'd often practised that expression in front of the mirror but its effect had never been all that great. My mother didn't notice it at all and Mick would look back at me, far more inscrutable than I was, until my eyelids flickered and I had to laugh.

'Good evening,' I said to the Indian, in my best Diné-Bizaad.

135

He looked at me for a long time, inscrutably. For a really long time. Finally, he crossed his arms, breathed in and out and replied, 'Good evening, Brother.'

'Do you understand me?' I exclaimed—again in Diné-Bizaad, of course. 'I bark, you bark, he/she/it barks?'

'Who's barking?' the Indian said.

'No one.' My heart leapt. 'I mean, it's splendid you understand what I'm saying. You're my first Navajo. I've learnt it all from books.'

'You can read?'

'He understands me!' I called up to the sky where stars, meanwhile, were shining. 'A Navajo, an honest-to-goodness Navajo, and he understands what I'm saying!' I performed something like a dance of joy, circling the Indian with wild leaps. 'You understand me!' I stopped before him.

'Of course I understand you, Brother,' he growled. 'That's crystal clear. It's just your clan, I can't quite put my finger on it at the moment.'

It was true: his glottal pauses were falling in different places from mine. Actually, he was making no glottal pauses at all.

'My clan is a small one,' I said. 'Two warriors, two squaws. I am a chief and my name is Running Deer.'

136

'I can see the mark of your majesty in your hair, Running Deer.' The Indian pointed at my feather. 'In me, too, you see the highest member of my clan. My name is Roaring Mountain Lion.'

The word he used was *dlozilgaii*, no doubt a lion from the mountains. A roaring one. But he pronounced it in such a very different way from me that I burst out laughing. I could hardly stop. 'Dlozilgaii!' I choked. The way he pronounced it—stressing the final vowel—made his name sound more like Brightly Coloured Squirrel. It took me ages to calm down.

Not even the corners of the lips of the Navajo Chief had twitched. He looked at me the way Indians do, simply. I wiped the tears from my eyes. We were silent for a few minutes. Time is different for the Indians and so, now, it was a new kind for me too.

'Those ones at the wall of the building,' I then said, pointing at the black-as-night city hall, at the top of the square. 'Were they from your clan?'

'You saw them?'

'Naturally.'

We were silent for another few minutes.

'I'm dying of thirst,' I then said, after all. I pointed at the brightly lit entrance to the bar, from which music was now coming, some hillbilly melody or other. 'May I buy you a beer?'

The Indian shook his head. He turned around, walked at a measured pace up to the city hall and vanished into the wall. Gone. The square was deserted. I gulped, turned around and pushed open the swinging door of the bar. The hillbilly music was now roaring.

The next morning, I got up at some unearthly hour. Not yet nine, it was. Nevertheless, too late. Booted and spurred, Mrs Miller was sitting on the stairs outside the entrance. She jumped up when she saw me. 'At last,' she said. She was buzzing with energy again. Stick in hand, she set off, taking large strides. Swinging my bone, I hurried along behind her. I wouldn't have minded a coffee from the machine.

The place wasn't much more than a pile of houses, resembling a no-longer-needed props room for Westerns. Wooden houses with swing doors. A draw well. Ground-level terraces with railings to which horses were tied. A car or two, as well, of course, none without dents, a smashed rear window or a bumper hanging off. Maybe the wreck outside the motel was still operative too.

At the edge of town, Mrs Miller headed for a hut with a corrugated iron roof, standing lonely among nettles and withered bushes, on the terrace of which a man was sitting in a rocking chair, entirely motionless, his eyes closed. A scraggy old man with almost no hair and a toothless, half-open mouth. Unclear whether he was still breathing, even. We stepped onto the terrace and stood before him.

'Captain Briggs!' Mrs Miller roared with a voice that would have wakened the dead. Captain Briggs wasn't dead, not quite yet, jumped up and was standing at attention even before he'd managed to open his eyes properly. His chair rocked to and fro.

'Present!' he barked.

'At ease!' Mrs Miller said, now much more quietly. Captain Briggs blinked, still half in a dream world we knew nothing about—and that was a barrack yard, probably. The other half of him examined us, suspiciously.

'My name is Miller,' Mrs Miller said. 'This is,'—she turned to me. 'You've never told me your name.'

'*Never mind*,' I said, in English.

'Never Mind. A beautiful name.' She turned to Captain Briggs again. 'Mr Mind and I intend to shed some light upon the Window Rock Revolt of 1938. Mrs Jamie of Jamie's Bar tells us you were present at it.'

'Me?'

'You are the last remaining eyewitness.'

'Witness?' Captain Briggs dropped into his chair and rocked, far back and just as far forward. His fingers, scrawny and full of blue veins, were clinging to the armrests. 'Never!'

Mrs Miller dug out a ten-dollar banknote from the folds of her dress and put it down on the Captain's left knee.

'I can't remember.' He closed one eye, but the other was squinting at his knee. The chair was no longer rocking.

Mrs Miller put down a second banknote, on his right knee. A five dollar. Captain Briggs opened his other eye again.

'It was a long time ago,' he mumbled.

'Right, that's enough!' Mrs Miller roared, at least as loudly as one of those slave drivers at West Point, with their bald square-shaped skulls and chins like spades. 'I want to hear everything. From beginning to end. Now.'

'You know the Navajos,' Captain Briggs muttered. 'Need to slaughter a few white men every now and then. Can't help themselves. We had to arrange for some public peace.'

'And how?'

'We showed the sows what's what,' Captain Briggs said, straightening up so quickly, the backrest thumped the back of his head. He didn't respond. 'A whole tribe, in full warpaint. Feathers, tomahawks, bows and arrows. Butchered whatever came under their knives, they did. Men, women, children. A bloodbath. Even Jamie, the first Jamie, had to believe it. The chief himself tore her to pieces. Ah, the Battle of Window Rock, how could I forget!'

'You were close to it,' Mrs Miller said.

'Are you writing for the paper?' Captain Briggs was wide awake now. '*The Flagstone News*?'

'Something like that.'

'Yes. Of course. The truth has to come out.' He clenched his fist and punched the other palm. 'I'm the last. You're very right there, Madam. High time it is that someone talked about the heroic battle of Window Rock. And who knows the truth apart from me!'

'On you go then,' Mrs Miller said.

'We kettled the Navajos in, on the square. You know where—where Jamie's Bar is. None of them could get back out. We fought with assorted weapons. Suffered considerable loss, we did—us too. In the end though, after a fair fight, we'd butchered the lowlives. Only the chief was still alive. In among the carcasses of his gang. A giant, truly, a giant with bloody, red teeth. He alone had killed a dozen of my boys. That's maybe why the troop was happy to leave him to me. And me alone. Man against man, in keeping with the custom and practice of old America. Me with my bayonet, he with his tomahawk and knife, both red with the blood of my comrades. No wonder I saw red too and raced towards this beast. My comrades—those still alive—formed a circle around us. To keep it short: the fight lasted for hours. But in the end, the last of the Navajos was lying on the battlefield too. Cries of hurrah from my comrades. I was carried around the square on their shoulders. Hats flew into the air. A grateful population dared to leave their homes again and streamed onto the square. I reminded the troop, naturally, that it's always all the soldiers together, never just one individual, who pass the test of battle. I simply had my role to play in the combat, it was God's will. Every single one of you, I said, would have done what I did.—No chance. I was now the hero. And it was true, there were a few comrades who'd

shat their pants with fear. — Roaring Mountain Lion was the
name of the lad. A mountain, even in death. He looked badly
savaged — he did, indeed — as he made his way to the Eternal
Hunting Grounds. We buried him in the middle of the square,
just.'

He fell silent. Then he put a hand on Mrs Miller's arm.
'Hand grenades,' he whispered, as if sharing a secret with
her. 'A hand grenade can work wonders is all I'm saying.'

He burst out laughing in a way that threatened to be
too much for his old man's body. He whistled and choked,
his skull turned red, the veins in his temples were swelling.
He sat there, screeching with excitement. We waited to see
whether he'd calm down, then left without a goodbye.
When we reached the square, we could still hear his whin-
nies. As if his horse had gone mad.

'He's a lying so-and-so,' Mrs Miller said. 'But he's the
only one who was there.'

'1938?' I said. And when Mrs Miller nodded, 'On 21
May?'

'How do you know that?' She stared at me.

I was suddenly in the best of spirits and about to clap
Mrs Miller on the shoulders. She realized this and stepped
aside. At the other end of the square, you see, were the

Indians, among them my chief too, Roaring Mountain Lion, or possibly Brightly Squirrel, whom Captain Briggs—if it had, in fact, been him—had indeed badly savaged. They'd started earlier than yesterday, or spent half the day, anyway, sitting around the scene of their defeat.

I walked—with Mrs Miller in tow—slowly across the square while the Indians, one beside the other, came towards us in just as measured a fashion. Now, in the bright light of day, I could see them more precisely than yesterday. Four Indians, one white man. They looked grim. One was a veritable scrap of meat, who could only walk because, in his world, the laws of gravity and human medicine no longer applied. In the Eternal Hunting Grounds, you can walk without legs too; float, with your bloody stumps just above the dusty ground. The cranial vault of the second was shattered. The third Indian, like the chief, was still halfway intact. All were feathered and painted in all the colours and tones of the earth. The blood, wherever you saw it, was as fresh and red as on the first day.—The trapper was with them too. He looked just as bad. A face that suggested he'd just fought ten rounds of a boxing match for which his hands, unlike his opponent's, had been tied behind his back.

We were now so close to each other, Roaring Mountain Lion raised his hand and stopped where he was. With him, the whole horde stopped. We halted too, Mrs Miller only because I held her back by the arm. She'd have run straight into the chief, otherwise. They were all standing now and looking at us, inscrutable also in death. The trapper had such puffy eyes, he could probably see just about nothing. All five stood next to each other beyond the odd flat hill of earth. We were on this side of it.

'Greetings, Running Deer,' the chief said.

I bowed my head. 'I greet you, Roaring Mountain Lion. And I greet you, brave warriors of the tribe of the Navajos. And you, too, white man.'

'I don't understand Diné-Bizaad,' Mrs Miller said. 'I told you already in the Mutz.'

'Don't be surprised by anything that happens in the next few minutes,' I said—in German, of course. 'By anything at all. Promise?'

'Okay,' said Mrs Miller. She stood with her hands on her hips, looking at me with eyes that were narrow slits.

I turned to the chief again. 'The Great Manitou decreed this,' I said, in my best Diné-Bizaad again and, in my head, recalling the chapter of Goossen's *Speak, Read and Write Navajo* entitled 'How to Tackle Tricky Themes'. 'He wants me to speak to you about the Battle of Window Rock, of which you are all heroes.'

The advice in my textbook had been correct. Invoke Manitou and then state the problem, making it crystal clear. Immediately, the chief began to speak, as if he had waited decades on such an invitation. He called the Battle of Window Rock the Massacre of Tségháhoodzání. Tségháhoodzání was the Indian name for the place where we were right now, once the very heart of the Navajos. A sacred place where, whenever there was a full moon, the heads of the clans met for a long palaver. Pasture routes were agreed upon, strategies for the battles against the Apaches and, soon, also against the first settlers on their way from east to west. Naturally, there'd been no city hall and no bar back then. No firewater either, and no Budweiser.

'It's all going really well,' I said to Mrs Miller in German, noticing that, despite my entreaties, she was about to lose her patience. She could only hear me, of course, and I was silent the whole time, apart from a few grunts of agreement and encouragement. That someone else was there and that this someone was unleashing a very un-Indian torrent of words, she couldn't hear.

'Okay,' she said for the second time. 'Okay, okay, okay.'

I figured out roughly the following from what the chief reported: the *army*—he used the English word—had decided—that must've been at the beginning of 1938—to use the area around Tségháhoodzání as a parade ground. Still the best pastures of the Navajos, back then. Armed troops saw to it that the Navajos could no longer erect their tents and the sheep had to graze in the mountains where there was no grass and the wolves killed the animals. Things went on like that for two or three months, the *army* shot around the requisitioned pastures with ten-inch rifles and flattened the grass with tanks. Up on the mountain ridge stood the Navajos, watching. They palavered and quarrelled and couldn't decide whether they should deliver a petition to the American president or the mayor of Window Rock, or attack the tanks on their horses (that said, they had at their disposal just three stallions, of which two were already really old) and chase them out of the country. Then, however, when on a hot day in May, an unexploded shell killed a boy who thought the silvery thing was a toy, the anger of the Navajos boiled over. They fetched all of their ancestors' props, which they'd looked after carefully but—apart from at tribe celebrations that seemed like folklore to them too—had never used, and all the fit-for-action men in the clan made their way to Tséghádhoodzání where the square already looked as it does today. There were eight warriors (the chief's clan was small too): three herders who looked after the sheep and were the most incensed as their animals, by this stage, couldn't find any grass whatsoever in the mountains; a petrol-station attendant who worked at an Esso garage in Fort Defiance; a barkeeper (not from Jamie's); a teacher at the primary school in Sawmill, a young man who did all kinds of work; an old man who otherwise just sat around the house; and the chief, Roaring Mountain Lion, who was the bus driver on the route down to the Interstate 17. He collected his dressed-up warriors on the bus (the morning timetable was cancelled) and drove them to the square in Window Rock where he pulled up at the usual bus stop outside the *city hall*. They were some sight for sure, the eight warriors, with their feathers in their hair, their warpaint, their bows and quivers full of arrows and their calumets on their belts. What exactly they intended, this foolhardy company, wasn't clear to them; wasn't clear to their chief either, to whom I was now speaking. (That there were now just four Indians was, no doubt, down to the fact that the successors of the other four had died on them, had been escorted, and so those four were now in an eternal stupor in the mass of faceless souls.)

148

The square already looked then as it does today. The bar existed too—Jamie's, the original ur-Jamie's. The warriors decided they needed some Dutch courage first and drank so much, they were soon seeing double, first themselves and then their opponents, who turned up at the bar in the form of the sheriff and his deputy. Four pale faces, armed with revolvers—from the perspective of the chief— two of whom had a star on the chest. They too ordered a beer each and began a discussion with their wobbly adversaries, the point of which was that gatherings of more than three Indians in Window Rock was inadmissible. Finish your drinks, pay up and off you go. Otherwise, the state would have to regard their behaviour as insubordination and take appropriate measures, having regard to the Restriction of Indian Rights Act of 1908, Articles 2 and 14b.

'We threw them out of the bar,' Roaring Mountain Lion said. 'Some time passed, a lot or a little, then there was a bang outside. When we looked out of the window, a troop of soldiers in blue uniform was kneeling in the middle of the square. They fired at the bar. Jamie rushed out and didn't return. We were shooting with bows and arrows and threw first empty, and later also full, bottles at them. The white men at the bar were complaining. And suddenly there was a loud bang, yes, and here we are.' He pointed at his men, this heap of human rubble.

I thought I now understood what had happened that day in May 1938. At the exact time when, a few thousand miles away, I came into the world. I told Mrs Miller what I'd concluded. She listened to me with ears that were getting redder and redder. Her eyes were even bigger and rounder than usual and her mouth was open.

The sheriff—thus began my summary for Mrs Miller—phoned the army base at Flagstone from his office. Help, insubordination, he needed military support. Some time passed: for the sheriff, slow-moving; for the Indians in the bar, imperceptible. Jamie served one beer after another while the Indians discussed what their next step should be. Storm the *city hall* or ride over to Los Alamos and destroy the newly built military installation. Perhaps they'd long lost sight already of the fact that they were on the warpath and were enjoying unexpectedly being together. The three white guests who were passing through and whom no one knew happily joined in the debate and made a few suggestions. Of them, too, only one—the one with the smashed-up face—was still allowed back up.

Finally, in the late afternoon, an armed troop arrived from Flagstone, twenty men perhaps, fewer than the sheriff had hoped (the Indians looked scary) but certainly enough to lead off the fight. The commander, he too a low charge, planted himself outside the bar with a megaphone and said it had to be vacated within a minute. Or else they'd open fire. At first, nothing at all happened—the soldiers stood ready for battle and the guests in the bar carried on palavering as before—and then the commander had a first volley fired. To frighten them. The shots did no damage but moved Jamie to rush out to ask the soldiers if they had gone mad. She was shot dead. Lay on her back in the sand. Now that all hell had broken loose, the soldiers wanted to storm the bar and were firing indiscriminately, the Indians shots their arrows through the window, causing the *army* to retreat. Again, it was quiet for a long time. The Indians were deliberating; the commander considering a better strategy. The one that occurred to him *was* better than his approach to date (or much worse, and horribly so). At any rate, he launched a pretend attack, face on, with lots of noise and gun smoke, while two of his soldiers (one of them, probably, Private Briggs)—unseen—crawled under the windows of the bar. Simultaneously ('Go!'), they threw two hand grenades into the bar and ducked down at the blockhouse wall. Everyone in the bar died on the spot. The three white men were collateral damage, though the term wasn't yet used at the time.

'Tallies with my research,' Mrs Miller said. 'I regard the case as closed. — How do you do that? Speaking into the air and you end up knowing everything about the Massacre of Window Rock?'

'It's a secret. I gave my Indian word of honour not to spill the beans.'

'Hmm,' Mrs Miller said. 'A-ha.'

Suddenly, the chief, Roaring Mountain Lion, stepped up in front of her. He convulsed his face to a grimace and emitted a terrible cry. Terrible and loud, the cry of the Navajos on the attack or perhaps their roar when they die. The chief stood close to Mrs Miller — so close, their noses were touching — and stared into her eyes. She couldn't see him, of course not, could hear his howling even less, but seemed to feel the whiff of cold air he brought: she put both hands round her upper arms and rubbed them.

'White men cannot see us,' the chief said, turning to me. 'White women certainly not. You can see us. Why?'

'That's why,' I said, taking the army-patent spade from my belt, flicking it open, and hewing it as hard as I could into the chief. It went through him as through a light curtain.

Exactly as I'd expected. Nonetheless, when I regained my balance, my heart was pounding. What if the dead man hadn't been dead? He'd then be dead now and I'd be his murderer.

'As I was saying,' the chief said. 'For a white man, we are nothing but air.'

'What are you doing, waving your spade about?' Mrs Miller said.

Again, I answered with my spade. I slammed it into the ground at the spot where the odd hill of earth began, this tumulus flattened by hundreds of cars driving over it. Everyone could immediately see a professional was at work and, suddenly, I comprehended myself why, for so many years, I'd—seemingly pointlessly—been digging up potato fields: in preparation for *this* moment. In Daphne Miller, I'd found, late enough in the day, my Schliemann, my Stamatakis, digging for whom was worth the effort. And now the fact I was unrivalled when it came to quick, precise work was paying off. Less than five minutes and before us lay an immaculate skeleton. Shiny skull, white bones, the arms crossed over the chest. On his skinless head, this dead man was wearing a feather headband, and on his body were hanging the remains of a leather garment. Moccasins, the bones of his feet still in them. The Indians and the white man crowded around and looked into the hole I'd dug.

'My headdress!' Roaring Mountain Lion exclaimed. 'My shoes. How does this man have them?'

'That's you.'

'But that would mean I was dead!' He laughed. Now the other Navajo warriors laughed too, as heartily as my textbook had told me to expect. There was even a chortle from the white man, from his blood-splattered mouth.

I continued to dig at the same clear and determined pace—and, less than ten minutes later, they were all lying there. All eight Indians, one next to the other, and the three white men. The dead souls clustered around their remains, trying—chattering like magpies now—to find themselves. Each soon succeeded as each had his own calumet on his belt that hadn't yet crumbled to dust; or a tomahawk with the familiar decoration; what remained of their trousers; his special feather headdress. The white man recognized his pocket watch, an onion-shaped thing that had stopped at half past eleven, covered in earth for the longest time, no doubt.

'Wow!' Mrs Miller said. Half of her was inside the chief as she stood, also looking at the bones, feathers, quivers and necklaces.

Two figures were approaching, diagonally across the square: Captain Briggs, in a wheelchair, and a hefty chap of about forty who was pushing him and had a star on his chest. The current sheriff. The two of them approached slowly and stopped beside us. The sheriff looked at the pile of bones, and Captain Briggs, at his feet.

'What's that?' the sheriff said.

'Eleven people killed by Captain Briggs,' I said. 'A life sentence, if you ask me.'

'Those are the guys.' Captain Briggs raised his head and sniggered. 'Blew them all away, I did. In a oner.' He beamed at the sheriff.

'Self-defence?'

'They'd no time to defend themselves,' Captain Briggs sniggered even louder. 'Boom, gone.'

The sheriff scratched his head. 'Too late in the day, anyhow,' he muttered, reaching for the handles of the wheelchair again.

'Not when murder is involved,' said Mrs Miller.

The sheriff gave her a look for which he should've got life too. Captain Briggs sniggered even louder. It was to be feared he'd start his whinnying again. The sheriff, also realizing that, pushed the wheelchair, at the double, towards the swing door of Jamie's. Without braking and Captain Briggs' legs first, he crashed into the door. It swung open, the Captain started to whinny—pleasure or pain?—and the two vanished inside.

The Indians now tried to gather their things up out of the earth—in vain, naturally. Again and again, the trapper, too, tried to get his immaterial paws around the watch. The chief was the quickest to comprehend his fate, straightened up and walked gracefully—without a glance at Mrs Miller or me—towards the blockhouse. He vanished into the wall. The others took a bit longer to concede defeat, then ran even faster behind their chief. They, too, were swallowed by the wooden beams of the wall. The square around us glowed.

'I need a gulp to drink now,' Mrs Miller said. My throat was burning too. We went across to the bar. In the doorway, I turned around again. The skeletons were lying in the dust, one beside the other, eleven skulls, staring into the sky through hollow eyes. Beside the head of the chief lay my spade.

We stood at the end of the bar, as far away as possible from the sheriff and Captain Briggs. Captain Briggs was red in the face and struggling for breath. The sheriff gave us a hateful look. Jamie, the current Jamie, pushed two Budweisers across the counter. We drank. 'Ahh!' Jamie was already arriving with the next two beers.

'Time for first names, I'd say!' Mrs Miller raised her beer can. 'I'm Daphne.'

'Cheers, Daphne,' I said.

'Here's to you, Never!'

We drank. I put the can back down on the counter and said, 'The name's Horst, actually.'

'Cheers, Horst.' She nodded, deeply serious, and took a gulp. 'No one's name is what you think it is. My name's Daphne, true, but I'm actually Bibi.'

'Bibi??'

'Bibi.'

I stared at her. Bibi! Was it possible she was Mr Adamson's Bibi? I calculated the dates—yes, she was an old lady, she could certainly have come into the world around 1934—and compared her facial features with those of Mr Adamson. Well, she wasn't an exact replica. But you, Anni, aren't my dead spit—and yet my granddaughter. The three

157

strands of hair on Mrs Miller's head very much reminded me of Mr Adamson's three sharply angled hairs. And her eyes! Basedow in her case, bulging in Mr Adamson's.

'Bibi,' said Bibi. 'The first person to call me Bibi was Kimmich the shoemaker. I was so fond of him! I wish I knew what became of him.'

'His name's now Brzldrk,' I said. 'Or Drzlhmsk.'

'Do you know him?'

'Yes. No, I mean.'

'I used to play hide and seek with him,' said Daphne, who was Bibi. 'I'd duck down behind his shoes and he'd hunker next to the workbench. He'd such funny eyes and always wore a knitted jacket. Something grey. He *loved* to play hide and seek, Mr Kimmich. He'd glow with pleasure. On one occasion, he didn't want to get up though I'd long since found him. He just lay there. Just lay there.'

'He was dead,' I said.

'Dead?'

'And he wasn't Kimmich the shoemaker. But Mr Adamson.'

'Mr Adamson?'

'Your grandfather!' I said. 'Don't you know that Mr Adamson is your grandfather?'

Bibi flashed her eyes at me. 'Oh, you want to hit me with my grandfather! If I tell you who my grandfather was, you'll keel over.' She opened a can — so violently, the beer spat up at her nose — and emptied it in a oner.

There was triumph in her eyes when she put it back down, with the other cans. 'But' — she put a sharp index finger on my nose and laughed — 'I'm not going to tell you who my grandfather was.'

'Heinrich Schliemann,' I said.

'Googled me, have you?' Bibi hissed, with a completely new expression on her face, raging. She grabbed me by the collar and lifted me so high, my feet were dangling in the air.

'Schliemann, Schliemann, Schliemann!' She waved me like a flag. 'Heinrich, Agamemnon, the whole bunch. Troy, Mycenae, they wouldn't settle for less. My father was even after Atlantis!' She'd her paws around my throat. Like a puppet on a string in his death throes, I was, the way my feet were going. 'Why do you think I married Mr Miller? At seventeen? I didn't want to hear the name Schliemann ever again. And I certainly had no intention of digging.'

She put me back on the ground and loosened her grip.

I could barely speak. 'I've been looking for you for sixty-five years,' I said nonetheless. 'I have a gift for you.

From Mr Adamson. A suitcase. Treasure.' I was burbling and had tears in my eyes.

'Treasure. From Mr Adamson.'

'It's a long time ago. You were four when he died.'

'Adamson.' Bibi had calmed down and was drinking her beer in calm little gulps. Despite that, this can was empty in a jiffy too. 'No memory of him.'

A sudden sadness seized me. This Bibi one before me had meant the world to Mr Adamson. And she didn't even remember him! I eased my bout of grief by drinking at the pace that seemed to be standard in this bar.

'You played hide and seek with Mr Adamson,' I then said. 'Don't you remember? With an old white-haired gentleman with an upper lip like this'—I shoved mine way out over my lower lip—'and a bald head with three hairs growing on it. Three hairs, like your three strands. You've his eyes too. It could be that you played in Mr Kimmich's workshop.'

Bibi raised her shoulders. 'Adamson? No.'

'What would you say to Knut?' I ventured.

Her face lit up. 'Uncle Knut!' she whispered. 'Of course. Uncle Knut. I remember him. He was only allowed to visit when Papa wasn't at home. But Papa was never at home anyway.'

160

She looked dreamily up into the pub sky. There were no stars up there, true, more likely spider webs and bat nests, but she beamed, quite enchanted. 'He told me stories about wild adventures. He'd found treasure. Exactly, I remember the story about the treasure. He told it again and again, now this way, now another.'

'You see,' I said.

She sighed. 'He was probably just an old man from that part of town. Lonely. Told little children great stories.'

'A braggart, you mean?'

'A conman for children.' She laughed. 'Yes. Uncle Knut. I used to go to Kimmich the shoemaker's with him. My God, how I loved him.'

'Kimmich the shoemaker?'

'Uncle Knut, stupid. As only children can love.'

I could feel a heat now filling my heart, dispelling the little misery there'd just been. I said, 'He loved you as only grandfathers can.'

Of course, I now told Bibi the whole story, from the very beginning up to the moment I found her. So, as far as the Mutz. Ach, Anni. If only I were Scheherazade. She got to talk for a thousand and one nights in a bid to save her life — and succeeded. If I'd the time she had, I'd now tell you again, you personally, the whole story you've just heard because I told it to Bibi, the same way, all in all. That's what every storyteller on the main square in Marrakesh or Baghdad would do. But this is no story from the Orient and so cannot save me. At any rate, I didn't omit a single detail as Bibi had to understand the goal of all that, and this goal was the garden of Mr Kremer's villa. The suitcase with the treasure in it. The place where I now am, trying to fill your recorder with what I'm saying. Two million giga-bytes, or whatever they're called. The thing is: *I* no longer have a thousand and one nights available. Maybe just a thousand seconds, and one for luck. The sun is a hand's breadth above the horizon. Who knows, maybe you'll show up soon. Sooner than . . . What?

So I told Bibi how I'd met Mr Adamson—here in the garden, on the bench where I'm sitting now—how I found out that he was dead and my future escort, how I— half intentionally and half a fatal error—ended up in the netherworld and how I got back out. I told her that Mr Adamson had told me that he and Sophia had had four blissful, loving days and nights in Mycenae, yes, exactly, and that Agamemnon, her good father, was the fruit of that love. A forbidden fruit and clearly a secret one. How Mr Adamson, with my help—he needed me, being dead—had

looked for her. How we'd been able — at the last moment —
to save the treasure. How this treasure — a suitcase, about
the contents of which I didn't know — was hidden in the
shed in the garden of Mr Kremer's villa, hopefully still was,
though more than half a century had passed meanwhile.
This was 2011, then it had been 1946, but the villa was still
there, exactly the same as it always was, even the boxwood
hedges had been trimmed the proper way when, on our
visit to the white lady's home two days ago — just two days
ago! — I'd seen them. Well. Once I'd handed over Mr
Adamson's gift to her, Bibi, my mission in life would be
fulfilled. The rest would be an encore. And, I added: I
believed every word Mr Adamson had said. If he said there
was treasure there, then there was treasure there. I didn't
tell her that I'd seen Mr Adamson and he'd seen her.

'Man,' Bibi exclaimed. 'If we get cracking right away,
we can make the morning flight.'

She went over to Jamie, who'd fallen asleep on her
bar stool, resting her head on the counter, shook her and
pointed at the empty beer cans with which, while I was
talking, she'd built a big pyramid. All Budweisers, among
which, strangely, a single can of a different brand had
landed. Schlitz. Like a flaw in a genetic programme. Had
we drunk all that, for heaven's sake?

'Put it on the tab,' Bibi said. 'We're in a hurry.'

Jamie, who'd been lost in a dream world and whose gaze was vacant, nodded. The captain and the sheriff were still there too. The sheriff was sitting on the floor, his legs stretched out before him, his back against the wall, sleeping. His breath was rattling from his half-open mouth, his bottom lip at the level of his chin. Captain Briggs was bent forward in his wheelchair. His eyes were open and he wasn't moving. Not a sound. Probably, he was dead.

Bibi, also when she was drunk, drove like a professional. The roads were empty, a purple twilight hinted at the morning on its way. We drove on the same route back, only significantly faster and ignoring every single speed limit. '40 miles maximum speed', there was no telling Bibi that. I sat next to her—without my seatbelt on, the pickup did have safety belts but they wouldn't lock in place—clutching my bone which, as it swayed to and fro, gave me a feeling of security. En route, on the Interstate 17, we saw—the reverse image of our outbound trip—the sun climbing from the horizon up into the sky and following us in a low arc to our left, first red, then yellow, then white and whiter. When we arrived at the airport in Phoenix, it was burning so brightly that even with sunglasses I wouldn't have dared to look up. But I didn't have sunglasses.

We already had our tickets, of course — Bibi had asked the Single Malt Circle for a return flight for her too — and there were indeed two free seats still. Business Class. Here, at the check-in, Bibi's charm didn't work as well as in Europe. Her suggestion that she and I be upgraded in view of our advanced age and our loyalty to the airline and as a symbol of a general solidarity of everyone with everyone else simply bounced off the lady at the desk who, without replying even, and with a stony expression, pushed the boarding cards across the counter to Bibi.

'Have a good flight,' Bibi said to me, in English, so audibly that the lady at the counter must have heard her.

We were both tired in any case, exhausted, and fell asleep even before the plane took off. We'd have done so even in Economy. I slept pretty much for the whole flight, I remember at best seeing brief images of a film, some deep-sea divers or other who'd discovered a sunken city. Bibi groaned next to me but was staring straight ahead, her eyes wide open. I slept for another bit and then we were already preparing for landing, half an hour before schedule.

The ZX was waiting just as obediently at the airport as the Toyota in America had done. When I put my parking ticket into the machine and — though this was a Swiss airport — it wanted twenty-two euros from me, Bibi said,

'Twenty-two bucks! So much!' Yes, she was back in Europe. Where cars cost something even when doing nothing.

We drove up to Mr Kremer's villa. A warm autumn's day, not spring as once before. No yellow fields of stubble, no swarms of sparrows picking at the remaining corn, no cows, no jackrabbits. Behind Mr Kremer's villa were now houses. One next to the other. Cast-iron windows on the ground floor, miniature palms in buckets at the front doors and, in the gardens, pools in which two not-all-too-big children could certainly splash around.

My old house and, this time too, no one seemed to be at home. A child's bike lay on the slab path that led to the front door. A bit farther off, Mick's house: overgrown, in the meantime, with trees and bushes. Ivy. Not a soul there either.

I parked the ZX outside the gate of Mr Kremer's villa but didn't even try to open it. Instead, I led Bibi along the garden fence—boxwood hedges, just as impenetrable as in the past—to the gap at the end of the garden where you could get in. The footpath was still there, thank God. The bench was still at the corner too, from which, however, the old ladies from the old people's home—if they did still come walking here — could no longer see as far as the water tower. A house with a flat roof blocked their — and our — view.

Somewhat excited I was, certainly, to be so close to Mr Adamson, who mustn't see me; and to the white lady, against whose wall I'd to press this time too. Now too, the wall for sure left, as before, chalk marks on my jacket and trousers. The gap was still there but had become so narrow, it seemed impossible to force my way in. I did it nonetheless, using all my strength and feeling the sharp branches scratch my hands and cheeks. I closed my eyes. The leaves around me were rustling. I pulled and pressed and then stumbled, suddenly free of any resistance, into the garden.

'I'll fetch an axe from the shed,' I whispered through the wall of leaves behind which, invisible to me, Bibi was waiting. 'I'll clear a path for you.'

Something rustled, and Bibi broke through the trees, upright, beaming, like a she-buffalo that doesn't bother about a bit of a copse when determined to get to her feeding ground. The steam coming off her, she stood beside me and looked around — as I was doing — at the regained paradise surrounding us.

The flowers were growing as they'd always done, as if there were no seasons here. The honeysuckle was sprawling in its corner. Rosemary, thyme, wisteria, azalea, like in my childhood. Blackthorn, fuchsia, geranium, campanula, snapdragon, phlox, lavender, meadow sage: all business as usual. The clematis, as beautiful as back then. The hydrangea. The thousand marguerites in the meadow were there too. The hibiscus, the oleander, the poppy. And at the front gate bloomed, as they'd always done, red and white roses. The grass was now up to my knees and not to my stomach. Who took care of this garden whose master was invisible? For now too the house — I was sure — wasn't lived in.

Of course, I peeked left and right to see if I could spot Mr Adamson. He wasn't there or if he was, was well hidden. With Bibi in tow, I went over to the shed. It was untouched, as I saw right away; at no point had Mr Kremer or his night-owl gardener touched anything. Everything was where it should be: the wheelbarrow, the hoes and shovels, the axe, even the water barrel, as full as back then. Dust and dirt, yes, but not so much of it, actually. Did things keep better here?

I cleared away the junk that, back in May 1946, I'd thrown over the case. Soon, I was seeing its leather. A sticker on it with the words 'Eden Rock'. A minute later, the case, free of its camouflage, was standing between the beams of the shed. I brought it down and placed it in front of Bibi.

'It belongs to you,' I said.

She hunkered before her gift, viewing it from all angles. The seal was untouched, no question about it. She took a knife from one of the many folds in her skirt, forced the red enamel off and fumbled around at the locks. She burst them open and pulled at the lid. Finally, it relented and the case was open. It was empty.

'That's why it was so light,' I exclaimed. 'The bastard! Mr Adamson! Nearly bloody kills me over an empty case!'

It wasn't empty. At its bottom, which looked as if it had been lined with something like wrapping paper, lay a letter. Yellowed paper, faded ink.

'Dear Bibi,' it no doubt began. And I thought I could also make out the signature: 'Yours, Granda.' The rest I couldn't read—it was also none of my business!—for Bibi was holding it in such a way, I couldn't see the secret. What's more, the writing was in Sütterlin script, something—to this day—I can decipher only with difficulty. Bibi was having trouble too, clearly, for she was taking a long time even though the letter was only a few lines long. Finally she raised her head and said, 'Really sweet. He says, with this,' — she waved the letter — 'I'll certainly have a golden future. All the best. Yours, Granda.'

Something caused me to look into the case again. Paper, the kind you use to line shelves or dressers. One corner was slightly raised. I pulled at it and was soon holding, as I fell back, a stiff piece of cardboard the size of the bottom of the case.

'Now look at that!' Bibi exclaimed, bent over the case again and lifting out a sparkling something-or-other. A headband tripping with gold, something like golden braids, a necklace made of a hundred gold links.

'Sophia wore that, your gran,' I said as Bibi tried to put the golden tangle round her forehead and neck. 'Back then, with Mr Adamson. That said, that's *all* she was wearing.'

The gold was now all flowing over Bibi's head and chest in the way it should. A sparkling body of water, flowing down her. She looked stunning. Where the fastener touched the back of her neck, however, dangled a tiny piece of paper on the chain. A price tag. EPA NEUE WARENHAUS AG, it read. The department store. Nineteen francs, eighty. I tore it off with a good tug — Bibi, looking down at herself and all excited, didn't notice anything — crumpled it up and threw it into the grass.

'Clytemnestra's jewellery,' I said. 'Genuine and the original. Mr Adamson was no braggart. As I've always told you.'

She nodded. 'That's how wrong one can be. He was no conman for children.' She beamed at me with those spherical eyes of her. She was glowing, was really beautiful.

Alerted by a warning call from my heart, I turned to look at the house. Did I see Mr Adamson's face disappear around the corner?

'Let's go,' I said. 'Away from here.'

I put the case back where it belonged and went to the garden gate. It was open, maybe it had always been open. I let Bibi climb into the ZX, holding the door open for her, as for a queen, the front door, true, but I did so with a reverence that wasn't feigned. She *was* a queen. Neither the red socks nor the mountain boots did anything to reduce her majesty.

As we passed the tram stop she said, 'Stop! I want to take the tram.' I stopped and she got out.

'Thanks,' she said through the open window. 'Here.' She gave me a handful of dollars.

'What's that?'

'Your wage for the second day.'

She went over to the stop. I saw her fiddling about with the ticket machine, then the 16 was arriving already, a modern motor tram, the green of which was brighter than the old one and had a tinge of blue. Bibi boarded and sat down by a window. The last I saw of her was her profile behind glass, an antique face, framed by blazing flames. I sat, motionless, at the wheel until the tram—and with it Bibi—vanished around a bend. Then I too drove off.

That's the end of the story of Mr Adamson. And of Bibi. I've never seen either of them since. Or let's say: that's *almost* the end. At the beginning of the actual end, this morning, you were present, of course. What will happen next, only the gods know.

I think you were a little amazed when I called you at an unearthly hour this morning—well, at ten; I remained true to myself—and asked you to take me in the ZX up to the hill where I spent my childhood. We'd just seen each other yesterday, on my birthday, and you don't want to be with your Granda *every* day. But I need you today: need you to drive me here—which you've done—and need you to find me. That will follow.

It's true that, at the age of ninety-four, I don't drive as safely as I did at eighty. My eyes — and the accelerator foot wouldn't switch so automatically to the brake any more. I didn't want, on my last journey, to knock down some old man crawling across the zebra crossing so slowly that I can't get past him. Or a child even.

The ZX was standing, as it has done for years now, in its tiny parking space next to the wall of the house. It had vanished beneath ferns, brambles, ivy and roses. Only here and there: a patch of dusty body shell, rouge cerise. On the windscreen was the motorway permit for 2018. I must have never driven after that, at least not on the motorway. I was glad you helped me to liberate my car. True, I tugged a little at all the green stuff but it was more pro forma. You really got stuck in and tore the roses and all the other plants off the roof and the bonnet. And yes, when with a lot of strength you removed a whole carpet of ivy from the rear window, we both saw the bone. Simultaneously. 'There it is!' I exclaimed. You know what you said.

I'd my summer suit on, a designer-label showpiece of a tailor in Bellagio, and didn't want to ruin it: that, too, explains my reticence when it came to freeing the ZX. It still fits me perfectly, the suit. Beige, almost white, made from a kind of silk. I may have to walk around in it for quite a long time still and I wouldn't like to look like Mr Adamson, or even Roaring Mountain Lion. Old men need to pay more attention to their appearance than young lads. Even baggy trousers and an unironed T-shirt suit those boys. — I put my feather in the last of my hair too. The bone had to come along too, of course, but it was already in the car. It could be that it had been there since my farewell to Bibi as I didn't ever miss it after that, just as little as I did the army-patent spade that got left behind in Window Rock. The feather, I didn't miss all those years at all. I searched for almost an hour this morning before I found it where I'd put it. In the second-top drawer of the desk, among the photos. I looked at a few of them: young Susanne, beaming. Heart-rending. Little Noëmi, sitting on a swing. You, a charming child, blowing a bubble into the air. And Bembo and Bimbo, two healthy babies, next to each other in the buggy. — No Bibi. I didn't take a camera to Window Rock.

Naturally, I packed your presents from yesterday: the bark from Susanne, the gingerbread heart from Noëmi, the drawing from Bembo and Bimbo, your bread and your wine, Anni. A Marqués de Riscal, *cosecha 2026*. I'm drinking it right now—from the bottle—wonderful provisions for the journey. Fourteen percent, a bit strong for a hot after-noon. Be that as it may.

Amazing — the ZX started right away. That hadn't been its forte in its younger years. On how many winter mornings did I sit behind the wheel, praying and shivering and listening to the slower and slower stuttering, morendo, of the starter motor until the engine — just as I was about to give up — started after all! A black diesel cloud behind me, enough to set off the maximum-emission-limit alarm.

The ZX produced billows of fumes just now too when you — with me on the passenger seat — manoeuvred it out of its foxhole. The diesel fog wasn't thick enough, however, to conceal my loved ones who had all — as if coincidentally — come out to wave us off. All four held their nostrils shut with one hand and waved a hanky with the other. Susanne smiled as tears rolled from her eyes, Noëmi was wearing an overall as she was repainting her apartment. And Bembo and Bimbo were shouting with glee. 'See you soon!' you called to them. I waved and smiled too. Could be, I was also fighting tears.

You can certainly drive, Anni. It must run in the family. Noëmi too, your mother, can drive like a taxi driver. She too gives a bollocking to anyone who continues when she has priority or anyone who takes a left turn without indicating. Just like you. I never do that, though. At the wheel,

I'm serenity personified. An *ARSEHOLE*! every now and then, sure. But rarely more than that.

We drove down the old routes, across the town, past the railway station, Margarethenpark, then up the hill and finally my childhood street. Nice weather, a perfect day. It's Friday today, incidentally, I just mention that in passing. Friday, 22 May 2032.

You let me out at the gate of Mr Kremer's villa. Twenty-one years have passed since I saw it with Bibi; and it's standing there just as we left it, so unchanged that I began to regard it as eternal. The boxwood politely pruned, the roof tiles shining cleanly, the metal gate with no rust. The tree, too—a black cypress—was neither bigger nor smaller.

'Should I come and get you?' you asked.

'Gladly. Come when the sun goes down. I'd be happy to see that first.'

'Okay, Granda.' You got behind the wheel again and drove to the turning bay at the end of the street—where Mick's house is—then you turned and, swiftly changing gear, raced past me. You signalled something with your hand and laughed. I watched you go. I was still waving when the ZX had long since vanished over the crest of the hill and the engine, that lovely diesel rattle, could no longer be heard. I'd the bone in the hand that wasn't waving. The presents were lying in a COOP bag. Your recorder was in there with them.

I was about to enter the garden of Mr Kremer's villa—through the main entrance, quite officially—when, in the distance, outside Mick's house, I noticed a man, an old man, walking with a stick and shuffling laboriously in my direction.

An ancient old man, truly! He was hardly making any headway. Something prompted me to go over to him. (I'm frail, true, as you know, Anni. But as I say, I can still do the hundred metres on a day like today in nine-point-nine even. Minutes, still. Clearly.)

The old man was wearing brown cords and a yellow-and-black tartan shirt. In his hair—snow-white—he was wearing a feather. His eyes were glazed.

'Mick?' I said. 'Is it you, Mick?'

'Don't know,' he said. 'Am I Mick? And who are you?'

'Mick,' I said. I was now sure he was Mick. The same voice, and the mouth was the mouth of that boy from before too. On one hand, however, he'd only two fingers left.

'I don't know any Mick,' said Mick.

'The garden of Mr Kremer's villa? Running Deer and Wild Storm? The time we stole cement for the fish pond? Do you not remember?'

'No idea.'

'You're even wearing your feather! Like me! And look, my bone! Don't you recognize it?'

'No.'

'*Tyrannosaurus rex*!'

'Cow, more like,' he said. 'No, I can't help you, sir. Good day.'

He raised a hand like the Navajos do—the way we imagined back then the Navajos did—and shuffled on, in the direction of my old house, in the garden of which a man stood, younger than us, snipping away at the flowers. I didn't know him. Of course not. Mick staggered towards him and watched him, with an uncertain look in his eyes, as he worked.

All right then. I entered the garden of Mr Kremer's villa. The gate was still unlocked.

Now my heart *was* beating a little. I felt anxious. It was possible, after all—because it was Friday—that Mr Adamson was ready—and had been, long since. That he'd been waiting impatiently, if impatience existed in his world, and if he wasn't more afraid that *I* could turn up too early. Too early for him.

But the garden was empty. The flowers even more splendid than before, if that was possible. The lilies, such epic saffron lilies, I was seeing here for the first time. Had Mr Kremer planted them for me specially? Black roses, massive peonies, though the time for them was long past? Yes, there were even alpine roses, my favourite flowers, and stone turmeric! How were these flourishing at two hundred and eighty metres above sea level? Laburnum — golden rain — pouring down into the grass.

Birds like back then or, even, more: a whole horde of goldfinches fluttering around, orioles, chaffinches, swallows, pheasants! The cuckoo was cuckooing again! And *of course* a few ravens were strutting about in the distance. From a little window beneath the roof, an owl was even blinking — though it was broad daylight.

I sat down on the bench. Unpacked my presents and put them beside me. I opened the bottle (of course, I remembered the corkscrew, Anni!) and took out your recording device. Turned it on and began to tell these stories that you'll hopefully listen to. At first, I intended it for everyone. Then, more and more, for you alone.

I'm still speaking, as you can hear. The sun is approaching the horizon which, here, is the top of the boxwoods. I'm gradually beginning to worry that you could turn up *before* Mr Adamson and that all three of us could end up in an unpleasant situation over me. You would accompany me back to the ZX and still, there'd be no Mr Adamson. You'd perhaps even drive home — this is the worst-case-scenario — chatting unsuspectingly the whole way, and they'd all take me in their arms again (Susanne drying her tears first) and I'd return the bark, the gingerbread heart and the drawing to my desk. The bottle, though, would be empty. You'd have to get me a new one by next Friday. But perhaps Mr Adamson would drop by on another day. Escorts with a job to do can go anywhere, any time.

Anni. I can see him. There — without doubt, he's beside the shed over there. In the shadow of the cypress, where the suitcase was. Now, Anni, I suddenly feel a bit uneasy. This non-stop talking isn't helping either to calm these flutters in my heart. The ground's swaying beneath my feet, yes, my breath's getting shorter and shorter. Can you hear it?

Mr Adamson is coming closer, calmly, but straight towards me through the high grass in which he leaves no trace. He still has that white skull, three hairs on it, an upper lip like the roof of a tram stop. His eyes. He's serious.